Damien watched her for a long, intent moment.

"There is one way to hold on to Plover Park."

"What's that?" Lee asked without too much hope.

"We could get married."

I've died and gone to heaven. Lee's lips parted incredulously as the thought shot across her mind. Then sanity prevailed. "Not a real marriage, I take it?"

"Would you like it to be?"

Legally wed,
Great together in bed,
But he's never said…
"I love you."
They're…

Wedlocked!

The series where marriages are made
in haste…and love comes later.…

Coming in November 2002

Jared's Love-Child
by
Sandra Field

Lindsay Armstrong

MARRIAGE ON COMMAND

Wedlocked!

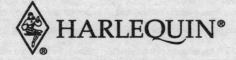

HARLEQUIN®

TORONTO • NEW YORK • LONDON
AMSTERDAM • PARIS • SYDNEY • HAMBURG
STOCKHOLM • ATHENS • TOKYO • MILAN • MADRID
PRAGUE • WARSAW • BUDAPEST • AUCKLAND

ISBN 0-373-12282-9

MARRIAGE ON COMMAND

First North American Publication 2002.

Copyright © 2002 by Lindsay Armstrong.

CHAPTER ONE

DAMIEN MOORE was tall, dark and unimpressed, Lee Westwood decided as she raised an enigmatic eyebrow after scanning her thoroughly.

True, she acknowledged inwardly as she sat in the chair he had waved a negligent hand towards, she was not as formally dressed as those who worked in the hushed and hallowed legal offices of Moore & Moore. But her newest pair of jeans, although not that new, were sharply pressed, her short brown boots were shining and her green blouse had been carefully chosen to match her eyes. In fact she couldn't remember taking as much care to co-ordinate her appearance for quite some time. Her shoulder-length auburn hair shone, as it always did, and was tied back neatly.

The one slightly jarring note was her old string bag, which she looped over the arm of the chair—she'd forgotten to change it for something more chic and, as usual, it bulged.

True, too, she reflected, that she had expected the senior partner of Moore & Moore to be older. This man was in his middle thirties at the most, she judged. Nor had it entered her expectations that he would be quite as devastatingly attractive, with lean lines, broad shoulders, clever dark eyes set in an intelligent face and a definite air of command. Well, perhaps that was to be expected, she amended her thoughts as he sat down behind a hugely impressive desk.

However, she wasn't going to allow this extremely good-looking but superior lawyer to intimidate her for any reason. And she said coolly, 'I need some legal advice, Mr Moore.'

He sat back in his exquisitely tailored charcoal suit and made a steeple of his fingers. 'So you informed my secretary on many an occasion, I gather,' he replied dryly.

5

'It's not easy to get an appointment with you,' Lee shot back. 'It's obvious you value yourself very highly, Mr Moore,' she added tartly.

A stray glint of amusement lit his fine dark eyes for a moment. 'My fees certainly don't come cheap,' he said, 'but if that's a problem for you I'm not sure why you persevered to the extent of driving my secretary up the wall, Miss…uh—' he consulted the file in front of him '—Westwood?'

'Well, I'll tell you, Mr—uh—Moore,' Lee parodied, 'I did some research and it seems to me that you are the best in the business. It's that simple.' She shrugged her slim shoulders, as if to say it was incomprehensible to her at the moment, but she would go along with it anyway, and added, 'I've got the strong feeling that's what I need, you see. On the subject of your fees, incidentally, I have a nest egg that should take care of them.'

Damien Moore resisted the urge to smile as he studied the snippy redhead seated opposite him. She *had* driven his secretary mad—no mean feat—and he got the strange feeling his wisest course would be to pack her off before she drove him mad. But really, he mused, how could a thin, young—twenty-three?—redhead, who appeared to have all her possessions packed into a bulging string bag, do that?

He sat up abruptly. 'All right, Miss Westwood, tell me what kind of trouble you've got yourself into.'

Lee looked pained. 'I haven't got myself into any trouble at all—I'm extremely law abiding!'

'So why are you here?' he asked impatiently.

'My grandparents…' She paused to collect her thoughts. 'They were persuaded to invest their life savings into a dubious investment scheme. Not only did they get no return for their money, but the principal has disappeared into thin air—the scheme was a scam right from the start,' she said intensely.

Damien Moore twirled a silver pen in his fingers and

looked sceptical. 'Firstly, why am I not dealing with your grandparents?'

'They...' Lee hesitated. 'They're the salt of the earth—they brought me up when my parents died in a car accident when I was six—but...well, they're rather unworldly. I guess,' she said awkwardly, 'that's why they fell for it in the first place.' Her expression hardened. 'But I intend to get back every penny they lost!'

'I see. That's where I come in, I presume?'

'To be honest—' Lee looked wry for a moment '—I was hoping to be able to achieve it on my own. I didn't succeed.'

'I hesitate to ask this, but what means have you already undertaken to get back your grandparents' life savings?' he enquired.

Lee threaded her fingers together and took her time about replying. 'I went to the police, but they seemed to think if there was any problem it was a civil matter. The contract contained the fine print to safeguard the proposer of the scheme, so I...' she grimaced '...I camped out on his door-step with a placard a couple of times.'

Don't laugh, Damien Moore warned himself. 'On the door-step of the man who allegedly conned your grandparents?'

Lee nodded.

'What did the placard say?'

Lee looked away. 'Basically, it was very uncomplimentary towards his integrity.'

'What did he do?'

Lee looked back at Damien Moore, contriving, he reflected, to be embarrassed but a picture of youthful dignity at the same time. 'He—that is to say, a member of his staff—threatened me with a restraining order.'

This time he had to laugh. 'I'm not surprised! I thought you were so law abiding, Miss Westwood—don't you know you can't go about impeaching people's integrity at will?'

'I happen to know,' Lee said stiffly, 'that he's a con man

and a thief! How would you feel if your grandparents were in the same position?' she asked burningly.

'All right.' Damien sobered and made a few notes on the pad in front of him. 'Who is this man?'

'Cyril Delaney.'

The silver pen dropped from his fingers and he blinked at her. 'You're joking!'

'No, I'm not,' Lee denied.

'Miss Westwood, Cyril Delaney is a respected property developer with a long-standing and impressive record. It is highly unlikely that he would be going around pulling scams on defenceless old age pensioners.'

'I have a document signed by a C. Delaney, I have my grandparents' word that the man they dealt with gave his name as Cyril Delaney, and I have their explanation that it was Cyril Delaney's ''impressive record'', Lee said with irony, 'that got them in. What do you make of that, Mr Moore?'

'That it was very likely someone masquerading as Cyril Delaney,' he replied promptly.

'Then he has a double,' Lee retorted.

A frown grew in Damien Moore's eyes. 'Are you serious—really serious, Miss Westwood?'

Lee looked heavenwards briefly. 'Do you honestly think I'd have gone to the amount of trouble I have on a deluded whim, Mr Moore? I've spent a fortune on phone calls alone, trying to get this appointment with you. You're only lucky,' she said, 'that your secretary gave in—otherwise I might have camped out on this doorstep!'

'Heaven forbid.' He looked at her coolly.

Lee grimaced. 'I can be determined and stubborn,' she conceded.

He studied her in silence for a long moment, then shrugged. 'I believe you. So you never got to meet Cyril?'

'No. I was fobbed off all the time. And then—well, I've told you that bit.'

'Have you put your claims down in writing to him?'

'That too, but I've received no reply. But he wouldn't reply, would he, if he was guilty?'

Damien Moore tapped his pen thoughtfully on his desk. 'It may have been interpreted as a crank claim.' He seemed to come to a decision. 'All right—show me your document.'

Lee delved eagerly into her string bag and produced it. 'What do you think?' she asked anxiously when he'd read it.

'That ninety-nine per cent of the population always fail to read the fine print,' he said witheringly. 'However, it would appear to me that some scam has been perpetrated, so I will write to Cyril Delaney and apprise of him of this document's existence—as well as the failure of the scheme.'

'And?'

He looked amused. 'That's all I can do at the moment.'

'What if he ignores you the way he ignored me?'

He raised his eyebrows. 'I doubt that will happen, Miss Westwood.'

Lee failed to look reassured. 'I really want to face him and have this out with him,' she said passionately.

'Yes, well, Miss Fire-eater, I don't know why that doesn't surprise me, but you'll have to practise some patience. We'll do this one step at a time—unless you'd like to find yourself another lawyer. May I have some details—where we can get in touch with you, et cetera?'

Lee subsided—until it became obvious that he required virtually her life history. 'I am not going to skip town without paying your fees,' she said proudly.

'Perish the thought,' he murmured, and threw her a keen, dark look. 'So you're a horticulturist? In what way?'

'I work as a landscape gardener, but my dream is to have my own business one day. I've always been passionate about gardens.' She looked wry. 'I've even dreamt about becoming as well known as Capability Brown was.'

It struck Damien Moore then that Lee Westwood's green

eyes were little short of stunning. Long-lashed and a clear jade-green, they were extremely expressive and—captivating. He also noticed for the first time that she was faintly freckled, and that her auburn hair shone with vitality. 'Uh…' he said, drawing his mind from her physical attributes. 'Have you seen any of his landscaping?'

A glint of mischief lit those eyes—a complete give-away—although she said demurely, 'Yes. I backpacked my way around the UK and Europe a couple of years ago. Have you?'

'No.' He didn't look put in his place, only amused. 'But my mother is a very keen gardener. She has books on him.'

'Are you interested in gardening, Mr Moore?'

'Not in the slightest, Miss Westwood. But…' He paused, and then surprised himself. 'If the way you're pursuing this matter is anything to go by, it seems likely your dreams will come true—I hope they do.' He stood up. 'In the meantime, leave this with me and I'll get back to you as soon as I have a response.'

Lee stood up but did not shake his proffered hand. 'Is that all?'

He raised a dark eyebrow and his mouth quirked. 'What more did you have in mind?'

For a moment Lee mistook his meaning. She even opened her mouth to say that surely they had enough evidence to do more than write to Cyril Delaney. Then she realised abruptly that his gaze had flicked up and down her body in a brief but unmistakable way—put plainly, in the way of a man asking an age-old question of a woman. Was she subtly suggesting she was ripe for the taking?

Her mouth fell open as comprehension came to her. Colour flooded into her cheeks and a burning sense of injustice possessed her. How dared this man think her capable of *double entendres*, or that she had any personal interest in him at all?

'You've got the wrong girl, Mr Moore,' she said arctically, 'if you mean what I think you mean.'

He looked faintly amused. 'It has been known to happen, Miss Westwood. And now, if you'll excuse me, I have a lunch date.' He pressed a button on his desk and right on cue his secretary opened the door and came forward to usher Lee out.

Lee's bedsitter was small but comfortable. Her couch doubled as her bed, and her compact kitchen resembled a ship's galley. But it was furnished brightly and attractively to match a glorious reproduction of Van Gogh's *Irises* that dominated one wall.

Normally her home soothed her, but that evening she was still unsettled by her encounter with Damien Moore as she ate her dinner: salad and an omelette. Not, she mused as she ate, that it was entirely surprising to imagine him being subjected to *double entendres* from women with more than business on their minds. Those dark good looks, the fact that he was obviously a man of considerable substance and his physique all added up to a dangerously attractive man.

What was more, he knew it—and not only that, he was perfectly capable of summing you up. And in her case, she thought a little gloomily, discarding you on a scale of one to ten of female attractiveness—to him anyway.

Then she had to grimace, because she couldn't believe this nettled her somewhat. Yet she was forced to acknowledge it did.

She offered herself some internal advice. If I were you, I would put Damien Moore as a man right out of your calculations, Lee. And if he doesn't come up with something soon—well, he'll hear from you, won't he?

She pushed her plate away and sighed. The nest egg she'd spoken of was small, and lawyer's fees would eat it away like a plague of locusts, she had no doubt. But she adored her grandparents, and the prospect of seeing them forced out of the home they'd lived in ever since she could remember was more than she could bear. It was also that home, in a country village three hours south of Brisbane, that had seen her green fingers come to light. Her grandmother was a passionate gardener and Lee had followed in her footsteps.

After leaving school she'd done a course in horticulture at the Southern Cross University in Lismore, not far from home, but then she'd had to move to Brisbane to find work. Her present job was with the city council's parks department, and she enjoyed it, but there was always at the back of her mind the prospect of owning her own business. As an adjunct to landscape gardening she was also interested in interior decorating; she'd done several night school courses in it. Her grandmother claimed that Lee was artistic, and could turn her hand to anything in that line.

Now, however, she thought a little sadly, until she got her grandparents out of this mess her dreams were receding a bit—unless Damien Moore fulfilled her expectations of being the cleverest lawyer in town. But, she reflected, even if he was, had she succeeded in getting him to take her seriously?

She got up to wash the dishes and decided she would give him a week.

Two weeks later, Damien Moore got out of his metallic blue Porsche at his favourite lunchtime restaurant to find his way barred by a slim girl wearing khaki overalls and with her hair crammed into a black crocheted hat. It was only when she took off the hat and a cloud of auburn hair settled to her shoulders that he recognised Lee Westwood.

He stopped and sighed. 'What are you? A one-woman SWAT team?'

'If you're referring to my clothes,' Lee said with dignity, 'they're my working clothes—I'm a gardener, remember? If you're referring to my presence here—' she looked around the Milton precinct, a trendy inner suburb of Brisbane '—I cannot get to you on the phone so I decided to do a bit of research. I knew you were coming here today.'

'How the hell did you know that?'

She smiled. 'Simple. On the phone I masqueraded as a legal secretary from another firm, desirous of getting in touch with you urgently on behalf of my boss. Your receptionist told me your movements just in case you'd switched off your mobile phone.'

Damien Moore swore. 'The reason you couldn't get hold of me was because I have no news for you. As my secretary would have informed you.'

'It's been two weeks!' Lee protested. 'If he was going to reply he'd have replied by now, surely?'

'Look—'

'No, you look, Mr Moore,' she interrupted, 'my grandparents had to take out a mortgage on their home to augment their pension and they're having trouble keeping up the repayments. If I don't get something done soon they'll lose their home as well—while you lunch out at expensive restaurants on my fees with not a care in the world!'

'Hardly,' he said, with a mixture of impatience and reluctant amusement. He seemed to come to a sudden decision. 'All right. Come and have lunch with me.'

Lee glanced behind her at the scarlet door beneath a straw-coloured awning flanked by tubs of flowering pelargoniums. It simply shouted luxury and expense. 'In there?' she queried cautiously.

'In there,' he agreed. 'I have a booking.'

'But I don't think I'm suitably dressed—there's a fast-food restaurant down the road—'

'Not on your life, Miss Westwood. Either in there or not at all.'

Lee chewed her lip. This time Damien Moore's exquisitely tailored suit was pale grey, and he wore a white and blue striped shirt with it, and a navy tie. His black shoes shone—handmade, no doubt—there was a navy linen handkerchief in his breast pocket and his thick dark hair was neat. There was also, she divined, the hint of a challenge in his clever dark eyes...

'OK.' She squared her shoulders. 'On one condition. That I pay for my lunch.'

'Why?'

'I don't wish to be beholden to you in any way, Mr Moore.'

He grinned. 'We'll see.'

Lee hesitated, but got the strong impression she might be left standing on the pavement if she crossed swords with him any further. So with a muttered, 'You're a hard man to deal with!' she took a deep breath and preceded him through the scarlet door.

Five minutes later she had a glass of wine in front of her and had ordered a slice of quiche Lorraine with salad—the cheapest item she could find on the menu.

'Are you sure?' he'd asked. 'You don't have to starve—'

'Quite sure,' she'd told him firmly. 'I happen to like quiche, and I adore salad.'

He'd shrugged and ordered the roast pork.

'This is very nice,' Lee remarked now, looking round. And I'm not sure whether it's because I'm with you, but no one seems to have taken exception to my overalls.'

He looked wry. 'I'm a fairly frequent customer.'

'So if I'd come in on my own it might have been a different matter.' She looked amused.

'As a matter of fact,' Damien Moore commented, 'you came in like the Queen of Sheba. It was quite an impressive performance.'

Lee laughed. 'Not the Queen of Sheba. A movie star.'

'Really?' He studied her quizzically. 'You were imagining yourself like that?'

'Yes.' Lee looked rueful. 'I don't usually have that problem, but you've got to admit I'm at a disadvantage today for this kind of place.' She glanced down at herself. 'Can I ask you a question?' she continued. 'Do you always lunch in such solitary splendour?'

He sipped his wine and she took the first sip of hers and

found it delicious. 'No,' he replied. 'Often it's a sandwich at my desk. I do work extremely hard, contrary to your thoughts on the subject, but I was supposed to meet someone today who had to cancel at the last minute. I decided to come anyway for a bit of peace and quiet. And the roast pork. Does that redeem me in your eyes at all?'

Lee looked momentarily guilty. 'Yes. Sorry about that! Who…? No,' she mumbled going faintly pink, unable to believe she'd been about to ask him who his lunch date was. 'None of my business.'

His lips twitched. 'It wasn't a woman.'

Lee could find absolutely nothing to say to this, and could only thank heaven that her lunch arrived at that point. Further deliverance came to her in the form of Damien Moore who proved himself to be, suddenly, a charming companion. As they ate, he drew her out skilfully on the subject so close to her heart: horticulture. And he told her about the little gem of a botanic garden he'd come upon in Cooktown, Far North Queensland, of all places.

How had he come to be in Cooktown? she asked.

On his way to Lizard Island, he told her, for some R & R. Did she know anything about the pink orchid that was the emblem of that small, remote but famous Queensland town?

It so happened she did but she was fascinated to hear about the botanic gardens, with their links straight back to Captain Cook and Joseph Banks, as well as the Chinese gardeners who had planted fruit, vegetables and flowers among the native trees and shrubs named by Banks during the boom times of Cooktown in the last century.

It was his mobile phone beeping discreetly that interrupted this discussion. He looked annoyed, but took the call. When he'd finished he looked at her enigmatically and said, 'It's your lucky day today, Miss Westwood.'

'Why?'

'I've been in court all morning so I've had no opportunity to see my mail. But Cyril Delaney has agreed to a meeting.'

The effect on Lee was electric. She sat up, her eyes sparkled with excitement and she said, 'Now we're getting somewhere! When? Where?'

Before he responded Damien Moore found himself once again intrigued by those green eyes. In fact, he conceded, there was a lot more to this thin redhead than he had first imagined. Stubborn and persistent, yes, but a plain nuisance was not exactly how he would describe her now, he thought, and narrowed his eyes. No, there was too much vitality. There was a hint of humour, and at times a rather touching dignity. Not that it meant anything to him other than in a lawyer-client context, he reflected. Or did it? No...

'In two days' time, at his home. He is not well, apparently, hence his delay in replying. He has also...' Damien paused and looked at the last of his roast pork thoughtfully '...requested your presence at this meeting.'

Lee pushed her plate away. 'Why do you sound disapproving?' she enquired with a frown.

His dark eyes were amused as they met hers. 'You do have a history of...inflammatory behaviour towards Cyril Delaney, so if I'm expressing any reservations it's to do with how you will handle yourself at this meeting, Miss Westwood.'

'Mr Moore,' Lee said, 'that will depend on how Cyril Delaney conducts *himself*.'

'That's what I was afraid of,' he said humorously. 'But histrionics only serve to put you in a more...vulnerable position.'

'You mean,' she said with a wicked little grin, 'they make people think you're all hot air and no substance? I would agree,' she added judiciously, 'most of the time. But there comes a stage when plain speaking is called for. So, while I won't set out to be discourteous I will certainly be honest.'

'I can hardly wait,' Damien murmured, and finished his lunch.

Their plates were removed, coffee was poured and a platter

of exquisite petits fours was presented. Lee took a miniature chocolate eclair and ate it with relish. Then she patted her stomach and sighed with pleasure. 'Definitely an improvement on the kind of lunch I had in mind, but sadly I have to leave you now, Mr Moore.' She consulted her watch. 'My lunchtime is just about to run out. Could you ask for separate bills?'

'Definitely not.'

'But didn't we agree—?'

'We agreed to nothing,' he said.

'Look, I would really like to pay for my lunch!'

'You might want to,' he said, 'but consider my reputation for a moment.'

Lee blinked at him. 'I don't understand. What has that got to do with it?'

'I'm not in the habit of allowing my guests to pay for themselves. Particularly not women.' His expression was grave but his eyes were another matter. They were full of secret amusement.

Lee gave it some thought before replying. 'Firstly, I don't think I fall into the category of a "guest".'

'I did invite you.'

She waved a hand. 'I didn't give you much choice.'

'Now that's an admission I didn't expect you to make.'

'Let me finish,' she ordered. 'Secondly, I'm not—'

'Not a woman?' he suggested, looking at her lazily.

Lee ground her teeth. 'Of course—but I'm not a *date*— and even dates can go Dutch anyway. But...look,' she said disjointedly, 'I resent being patronised like this!'

'On the contrary,' Damien Moore drawled, 'I've enjoyed my lunch today much more than I expected to—thanks to you, Miss Westwood. So I feel the least I can do is pay for yours.'

Lee stared at him wordlessly with confusion etched clearly in her green eyes. 'You have?' she said at length.

'I give you my word.'

'Why?' Lee asked.

He shrugged. 'You're full of surprises.'

'Like a circus act?' she suggested with some bitterness.

He laughed. 'No. Like a snippy redhead who shoots from the hip. It's rather refreshing.' His expression changed for a moment, as if he was viewing a phenomenon new to him. Then he said lightly, 'So let's have no more argument on the subject of who pays for this lunch.' He stood up.

But it took Lee a moment or two to follow suit, because something struck her as she stared up at the tall figure of Damien Moore—something rather stunning and almost enough to take her breath away. *Could you fall in love with a man over lunch?*

At two o'clock the next morning Lee gave up trying to sleep on her convertible couch and made herself a cup of tea.

She was still stunned and uncomprehending at the thought that had crossed her mind just before she'd left the restaurant with her lawyer. Where had it come from? What had prompted it? How could something like that leap into her mind on only the second occasion she'd met a man?

But even if she were able to answer those questions what difference would it make? she wondered. Nothing could change the fact that her articulacy had deserted her as they'd walked out into the sunlight and he'd asked where she was parked. She'd pointed to her car and he'd escorted her to it.

She'd thanked him awkwardly for lunch and agreed to meet him in two days' time, but it had been as if all the spontaneity and fluidity had drained from her—to be replaced by a keen awareness of the man beside her. The fact that his height caused a flutter along her nerve-ends, for example. The fact that she had enjoyed her lunch and his company much more than *she'd* expected to because he'd gone out of his way to make it enjoyable.

The fact, she thought hollowly, that he'd escorted her to her car as if he were escorting a movie star to her limousine rather than Lee Westwood in her work overalls to her second-hand yellow Toyota with its several dents.

But, she cautioned herself, with a sense of *déjà vu*, was it so surprising that at least a little flutter of attraction should cross her nerve-ends? How many other girls wouldn't have felt the same beneath the spell of a tall, good-looking man at his charming best?

And there lies the rub, she thought ruefully. She was only one of a long line, she had no doubt. She heaved a sigh and decided the last thing she should ever do was give Damien Moore any indication that he'd been right about her that first day in his office. And she made a mental note that this was the second time she'd issued a warning of this nature to herself.

They met outside Cyril Delaney's Balmain home on the appointed day.

Lee had taken the afternoon off work and wore neat beige linen trousers with a white shirt and a russet waistcoat. Her hair was loose but her trademark string bag remained the same. She showed no tendency to want to linger on the pavement, which Damien Moore noted, and he concluded from her severe expression that it held embarrassing memories for her.

He was tempted to ask her if that was so, but restrained himself. He had no real expectations of this interview solving anything for Lee Westwood's grandparents, and it had caused him a few minutes' internal interrogation to establish why that should concern him—minutely, but none the less it concerned him. The answer he came up with was that this feisty girl intrigued him. Not a good footing for lawyer-client relations, however, he reminded himself. *Don't get personally involved,* in other words…

A housekeeper showed them into a sun room at the rear of the large, luxurious house, and introduced them to a frail-looking old man in a wheelchair—Cyril Delaney. They all shook hands and Lee and Damien seated themselves side by side on a cane settee.

'So,' Cyril said, 'you're the young lady my staff had to threaten with a restraining order while I was in hospital?'

Lee moistened her lips but took her time. In his prime, Cyril would have been tall and angular, she decided, whereas now he was stooped. His features were narrow and his teeth prominent. A few strands of silver hair were carefully combed over his head. But his eyes were bright blue and shrewd.

'I am,' she said quietly, 'but I didn't realise you were in hospital.'

'Does that mean you would have picketed the hospital?' he enquired.

Lee coloured faintly. 'No. But I just couldn't find any other way to bring this to your attention, Mr Delaney, and I feel I am quite within my rights to at least get a hearing.'

'Hmm. So you've hired yourself a hotshot lawyer now?' He turned those shrewd eyes on Damien. 'Knew your father and I've always been an admirer of your mother, Damien Moore.'

'Thank you, sir,' Damien replied, and let a few moments elapse. 'Concerning Miss Westwood's claims on behalf of her grandparents—'

'Let the girl speak for herself,' Cyril Delaney broke in.

Damien turned to Lee with a clear warning in his eyes—*no hot air!*

Lee swallowed. Then she began to outline her grandparents' plight, coolly and simply. She concluded by saying, 'It was your reputation that got them in, Mr Delaney.'

Cyril Delaney lay back in his wheelchair. 'Piffle,' he remarked.

'Now look here—' Lee began, but Damien put his hand over hers.

Cyril noted this, as well as noting how Lee Westwood looked up at Damien Moore with a stubborn light in her green eyes, and how, when she transferred that stubborn green gaze back to himself, and repeated herself, Damien Moore's expression became tinged with a sort of wry affection rather than exasperation. All of which caused him to make a mental note concerning Evelyn Moore's good-looking son who as yet, he believed, had not been snared and taken to the altar.

Then he closed his eyes and overrode what Lee was saying so hotly.

'Young lady, tell me a bit about yourself.'

Lee stopped, open-mouthed. 'Why?' she got out at last.

'You interest me, that's all. And since I've been confined to this accursed wheelchair a lot of interest has gone out of life for me, I can assure you.'

This time Lee responded to Damien's pressure on her hand. 'Well...' she said a little confusedly, but didn't seem to know how to go on.

'Miss Westwood was brought up by her grandparents after her parents were killed,' Damien put in.

'Where?'

Lee told him, and received a suddenly acute look from the old man. 'Is that a fact?' he said slowly. 'And what do you do with yourself?'

Lee told him.

'You could be looking at the next Capability Brown,' Damien put in at the end of Lee's recital. 'Her tenacity is little short of amazing.'

'Don't tell me she camped out on your doorstep too?' Cyril hazarded.

'I did not,' Lee intervened, and pulled her hand out from Damien's. 'I would also appreciate it if you two would stop talking over me as if I didn't exist.'

Damien shrugged and looked down at her with a faint smile. 'There's little likelihood of that.'

'Hear, hear,' Cyril contributed, but in a curiously meaningful way that caused Damien to suddenly eye him curiously.

But Cyril seemed to tire abruptly. 'When's this damn document dated?' he asked testily.

Damien told him.

'I was in hospital. Someone was using my name and forging my signature. It's the only explanation, Miss Westwood. I'm sorry, but...' He paused, and frowned, then said almost to himself, 'No. Uh, I can certainly prove I was in hospital at the time, but you're welcome to inspect my bank accounts, Damien Moore.'

'That won't be necessary, sir,' Damien said.

'Just a minute,' Lee said desperately. 'I'm sorry, sir—I can see you don't feel well—but the man they described to me looked a lot like you!'

There was a sudden silence. And for a moment Cyril's gaze was electric blue on Lee. Then it became hooded and he said to Damien, 'Take her away, my boy, and look after her. And call the nurse on the way out.'

'Feeling better?'

'Yes. Thank you.' Lee put away her handkerchief. They were in a hotel bar not far from Cyril's house, and she had taken several sips of a strong brandy and soda. She hadn't quite dissolved into helpless tears on Cyril's doorstep, but there was no doubt she'd had tears in her eyes and been inwardly distraught. To such an extent that Damien had put her in his car and found this dim and quiet lounge bar.

'Sorry,' she said, taking another sip. 'It's the *disappointment*—and on top of that I feel *guilty*. He seemed so old and frail—I don't think it could have been him but there I was accusing him...' She ran out of breath and could only shake her head helplessly.

'I quite understand,' Damien murmured, 'but you're right, Lee. It couldn't have been him, although you weren't to know that.'

'So who was it?' She raised her eyes to his. 'And why did I get the feeling at the last moment that…I don't know…something I said made him stop and think?'

Damien studied his own drink with a frown. 'I got that impression too, but…' He shrugged. 'We may never know what it was.'

'So what now?' she asked.

'Lee, there's only one thing we can do now—hand it over to the police.'

'I tried that,' she said barely audibly. 'I told you.'

'Yes, but we've now established that even if the contract was watertight someone was masquerading under a false name, which could nullify it.'

Her shoulders slumped.

'I'll do it for you,' he said.

She looked at him and smiled painfully as a beam of late-afternoon sunlight came through a high window and formed an aureole of light around her auburn head. She was still pale, he noted, which caused her freckles to be more noticeable. Then she straightened her shoulders and took a deep breath. 'Thank you. But the truth is I can't afford you any longer, Mr Moore, so I'll do it myself.'

'Damien,' he responded. 'And I won't charge you.'

'I couldn't accept charity,' Lee said with another painful little smile, 'but thank you for the offer.'

'There's nothing you can do to stop me.'

Her eyes widened on him, seated across the small round table from her. At three in the afternoon the bar was empty except for themselves. So apart from the barman, who was energetically polishing glasses, there was no one to witness her reaction to the high-handed statement Damien Moore had just made.

'What do you mean?' she asked carefully.

He twirled a cardboard coaster between his long fingers. 'Every citizen has a duty to report a felony. That's what I'll do.' He shrugged, as if to say 'simple', but there was something in his eyes that indicated he wouldn't take no for an answer anyway. 'So there's no need to feel beholden to me in any way, Lee.'

She opened her mouth to argue this, but he grinned suddenly with so much humour that she literally felt herself going weak all over beneath the sheer attractiveness of it—and couldn't think of a thing to say.

'Well, that's sorted, then.' He looked at his watch. 'If you're feeling better now, I'll take you back to your car.' He paused and studied her intently for a moment. 'All is not lost yet, Lee. Hold on to that.'

She found her voice at last. 'Are you doing this because Cyril told you to take care of me? And why would he say that anyway?'

He raised an eyebrow. 'Who knows? I'd say he admired your pluck and felt for your grandparents' plight.' He hesitated, then, 'That's all.'

He stood up and Lee followed suit, looking dazed.

It was as he took her arm to usher her out of the bar that Damien Moore examined his slight hesitation and realised he was not at all sure that what he'd said was the whole truth. True, most people *would* admire this girl's pluck, even a sick old man. But he'd sensed something more behind Cyril's parting remarks; he'd almost sensed a judgement being made, on himself and on Lee, but what the hell it could have been he had no idea.

Unless… He posed a question to himself. Unless Cyril had divined that a slightly protective feeling had wormed its way into his relations with this client?

Out on the pavement, he stopped briefly and studied his client in the bright sunlight. She was obviously more composed now, although still pale, but he wondered how long she would remain so unnaturally quiet. He didn't have long to wait.

'Thank you very much for all you've done, Mr Moore,' Lee started to say. 'I really—'

'It's Damien, Lee.'

A fleeting tinge of exasperation clouded her gaze. 'I really appreciate your help and everything,' she continued stubbornly, 'but—'

'Just hop in, Lee,' he advised, and opened the door of the Porsche for her. 'I'm running late.'

'But I need to—'

'You don't need to say a thing. Go back to your gardens and leave this to me.' He patted the top of her head.

Lee bit her lip, now not only exasperated but all mixed up.

She took his advice and five minutes later she'd been returned to her car and he was about to drive off.

'I'll be in touch!' were his last words before he drove off, leaving her prey to a cauldron of emotions.

He was as good as his word.

Over the next few weeks he rang her several times, and invited her to have breakfast with him at his apartment once, to update her on the progress he was making. Then he took her to lunch to explain that it was going to be a long process, because whoever had masqueraded as Cyril Delaney had covered their tracks most efficiently.

During these meetings Lee was able to hide the ambivalence of her feelings towards him. She even felt she'd managed to revert to the snippy redhead who shot from the hip rather than the confused unhappy girl of the day of Cyril's interview. The girl who had, in the same breath, been both entirely exasperated by his high-handedness and then suffered a vision of how heavenly it would be to have Damien Moore looking after her...

A month later she read that Cyril Delaney had died after a long illness. She felt touched by sadness. But three days afterwards, when Damien rang her to tell that they featured jointly in Cyril's will, her emotions defied description as he explained the extraordinary bequest that was to change her life for ever.

CHAPTER TWO

DAMIEN MOORE looked at his watch, then glanced around the colourful pavement café impatiently. He had another appointment at two o'clock, now only fifty minutes away, and Lee Westwood was late.

He reached for the menu. She might eat like a rabbit but he didn't, and he had no intention of bolting down his lunch. So he signalled the waitress and ordered a steak for himself, a Caesar salad for his guest, and a pot of coffee.

'She'll be here shortly, I assume,' he told the waitress, 'and she always orders rabbit food so I can't go wrong with a salad.' He smiled at the girl but felt his teeth set on edge at being on the receiving end of a coy, simpering smile in return. Which prompted the thought that Lee Westwood might be highly exasperating at times, but at least she never simpered over him or batted her eyelashes at him.

Then he saw her approaching from way down the block. Her long auburn hair was flying, and so was the green scarf she had round her neck, as she loped along the pavement with her trademark stride in a pair of short leather boots worn with faded jeans, a large cyclamen T-shirt and a bulging string bag hanging from her shoulder.

Sartorially a disaster, Damien Moore mused, as so often—although he supposed he should count himself fortunate she wasn't wearing the black crocheted hat she often favoured, crammed onto her head.

OK, it was a pavement café, he told himself, but it was an extremely chic one, with its striped awnings and potted trees—which she would have known. And so was the clientele chic. Most of the women here looked as if they'd stepped straight out of *Vogue*. But when had that worried this girl, he thought amusedly, who could turn herself into the height of glamour on a whim? And, more to the point, what was it she possessed that still made her turn heads as she got closer?

Wonderful hair? Yes, he conceded. Long-lashed sparkling green eyes? Definitely a plus. Otherwise? That hint of freckles? He thought he knew enough about women to know they'd rather not be freckled—so a minus on the part of the beholden as well as the beholder, although he himself didn't mind Lee's freckles for some strange reason. A thin figure? Another minus, surely? Mind you, very long shapely legs...

But it wasn't any of the above plusses or minuses, he decided in the last moments before she arrived at the table. It was her sheer vitality and the aura that she didn't give a damn about what anyone thought of her. It was, after all, that force within her that had persuaded him to take on her legal battles when he'd known—and told her—she was barking up the wrong tree, and when he'd strenuously doubted that she could afford his fees.

'Sorry I'm late,' she said breathlessly as she looped the string bag over the back of the chair and plonked down onto it. 'The traffic was unbelievable!'

'Has it never occurred to you, Lee, that a bit of forward planning might relieve you of the tiresome business of having to apologise for being late?'

'Oh, dear!' She looped her hair behind her ears and glinted a laughing look at him out of those green eyes. At the same time she took in his severely tailored navy suit, pale blue shirt and discreet tie. 'Have I seriously offended you?'

He shrugged. 'Being late can make things difficult for other people. For instance, I now have only forty-five minutes to brief you.'

She gestured. 'That's only fifteen minutes less than you would have had if I'd been on time, not exactly an eon. I'm sure you can pack a powerful lot of briefing into three quarters of an hour, Damien, although I can't imagine what you need to brief me about anyway—oh!' She looked up as a huge Caesar salad was placed in front of her. 'You ordered for me!'

Damien studied the steak he was presented with, observed from the pink juices running from it that it was rare, as he'd requested, and picked up his knife and fork. 'If you'd been on time you could have ordered for yourself. Isn't that the kind of meal you generally go for?'

'Well, yes,' Lee conceded, but not in a conciliated manner. 'I would have asked for a much smaller one than this, though. I would have requested no anchovies, which I hate, and—'

'Don't eat the anchovies and leave half of it,' he recommended dryly.

'You don't understand,' she murmured, favouring him with irony in her eyes. 'The sheer size of a meal, however delicious, can be off-putting and take away your appetite.'

He swore. 'It's only a salad, for crying out loud! I'm not trying to force feed you a gargantuan serving of…of roast beef and baked potatoes. It wouldn't hurt you to eat a bit more either.'

'Is that designed to make me feel uncomfortable about my figure? If so, may I enquire what it has to do with my lawyer?' She looked at him haughtily.

Damien Moore breathed deeply—and counted to ten for good measure. Neither of these devices helped, however. For a twenty-four-year-old girl she often packed quite a punch, and was capable of needling him with the best. 'Nothing on earth,' he said coolly—and pointedly.

Lee grimaced. 'Then perhaps you'd like to tell me why you're in such a bad mood? Incidentally, I didn't just drive across town for lunch. I came up the Pacific Highway, which is undergoing considerable roadworks, hence the build-up of traffic and the delays.'

Something even more irritated flickered in his dark eyes, but almost immediately gave way to a form of self-directed irony. He eased his shoulders and said ruefully, 'Sorry. How's it going ''down on the farm''?'

Lee's eyes lit up. That little phrase 'down on the farm' encapsulated the miracle that Cyril Delaney's will had brought to her life. For the most bizarre reason he had left a property—Plover Park, its twenty-five acres and registered wholesale nursery—to her and Damien jointly, on the condition that they didn't attempt to dispose of it within twelve months. At one stroke it had not only brought her life's dream within her grasp but also, because of the income the nursery generated, it had solved her grandparents' immediate cash-flow problems.

The other part of the miracle was that Plover Park was ten minutes' drive from her grandparents' home—it was in the area where Lee had grown up and gone to university. It had been like going home for her. And her still active grandfather was more than happy to work the nursery with her.

'It's…fantastic,' she said glowingly. 'Sometimes I have to pinch myself! We're almost into full production now.'

He looked impressed.

'So what did you want to see me about so urgently?' Lee asked blithely as she inspected her salad and removed the anchovies.

Damien paused and wondered if there was any kind way of breaking the news to this glowing girl. 'There's been a complication,' he said slowly, and decided it was best to get it over fast. 'The will is to be contested.'

Lee gasped and paled. 'You're joking!'

He shook his head.

'On what…on what grounds?'

'On the grounds that we may have exerted undue pressure on Cyril to force him to make the bequest.'

'But we didn't! We had no *idea* it was going to happen,' she protested.

'You know that and I know that, Lee. Unfortunately Cyril is no longer with us to corroborate it.'

'And you…you set aside an *hour* of your precious time to break this news to me!' Lee stammered.

He shrugged. 'I'm extremely busy at the moment. And so, you gave me to understand, are you.'

'But this is terrible! It could be catastrophic!'

'It could indeed,' he agreed. 'For you.'

Lee stared at the Caesar salad she now definitely didn't want and swallowed. 'So what's your considered opinion? As a lawyer? Have *they* got a leg to stand on?'

Damien ate in silence for a while, then pushed his empty plate away and reached for the coffee pot. 'In general terms you're allowed to make bequests in your will as you see fit, provided your legal heirs are taken care of. One of Cyril's legal heirs,' he said significantly, 'has decided that he wasn't sufficiently taken care of and that Plover Park is rightly his.'

'Which one?'

'His brother. One of his contentions is that Plover Park belongs in the Delaney family. It was originally owned by their grandfather and has been in the family all that time. Whereas the only use we have for it is to sell it when the twelve months are up and divide the profits.'

'He…well, he's right—hard though that's going to be,' Lee said unguardedly, 'but how can he be so sure?'

Damien studied her searchingly for a long moment. 'Cyril wrote a letter that is on public record explaining this unusual bequest.'

'Try bizarre,' Lee suggested. 'But, whatever, I was completely stunned.'

'It was the last thing *I* expected. Nor did either of us, I would imagine—' he looked at her sardonically '—anticipate the explanation he left in the letter: that he had formed the opinion we were well suited and his dearest wish was that owning this property jointly would encourage us to marry and enjoy the benefits of Plover Park together.'

'You're not wrong,' Lee agreed in a heartfelt way. 'I nearly fell off my chair all over again. But—'

'Because we have given no indication that we intend to enjoy Plover park *together*, Lee,' Damien interrupted deliberately, 'Cyril's brother contends that we misled an old man who was virtually on his deathbed into leaving the property outside the family—do you understand?'

Lee blinked several times, then with a heartfelt sigh poured herself a cup of coffee. 'I had the feeling this was just too good to be true. That must be why I feel like pinching myself so often.'

'You perceive yourself to be morally wrong in the way you've interpreted Cyril's bequest?' he enquired with a lift of an eyebrow.

'I...' She paused. 'I will never know *why* he made the bequest in the first place, for one thing.'

'You got to him in the end, Lee. He obviously admired you.' A humorous glint lit his dark eyes. 'Despite the number of times you camped out on his doorstep waving placards impeaching his integrity.'

'If that's so,' she retorted, 'why didn't he bequeath Plover Park directly to me? Why did he have to involve you?'

Damien shrugged. 'He was dying, he was a bachelor—perhaps he regretted not having children like us to leave his wealth to. Who knows what his thoughts were in those last days? Or...' He paused and gazed at Lee narrowly. 'He genuinely did believe you and I were made for each other and we simply required a shove in the right direction.'

'How *could* he have formed that opinion?' she asked, looking baffled. 'There was nothing remotely lover-like between us.'

Damien put his head on one side and his lips twitched. 'How right you are. I spent most of my time trying to shut you up.'

Lee bit her lip. 'I thought—well, you know what I thought, and how much I love my grandparents.'

Something softened in Damien Moore's eyes for a moment but he said nothing.

'How do *you* feel about it all now, Damien?' she asked at length.

He took his time, then shrugged. 'The same as you. A sense of mystification. But we both felt that Cyril left something unsaid that day, didn't we?'

Lee's mind flew back as she sipped her coffee, and she nodded.

'Well,' he went on, 'Cyril Delaney had quite an impressive record, not only as a property developer but also as a philanthropist. It's become my considered opinion that he saw the bequest as a means of solving your grandparents' plight as well as making sure I was on hand to steer you through the pitfalls of it all.'

Lee's eyes widened. 'He did say...*look after her*...didn't he?'

'He did,' Damien agreed—rather dryly, Lee thought. 'Unfortunately that is only a theory, and not something I could prove in a court of law.'

'So...' Lee's hands trembled around her coffee cup and those marvellously expressive green eyes were bleak and sad. 'So it *was* all too good to be true.'

He watched her for a long, intent moment as she blinked urgently to hold back the tears. 'Not necessarily,' he said at last. 'There is one sure way to hold on to Plover Park.'

'What's that?' she asked without much hope.

'We could get married.'

I've died and gone to heaven. Her lips parted incredulously as the thought shot across Lee's mind. Then sanity prevailed. 'Not a real marriage, I take it?'

'Would you like it to be?'

She licked her lips, her eyes huge and stunned. 'We...we barely know each other,' she stammered. 'Uh...there's no way you'd even suggest this if it weren't for the circumstances, I'm sure! I think you must have been joking,' she added, with a mixture of dignity and a tinge of annoyance.

'Not in very good taste, if you don't mind me saying so, Mr Moore.'

He looked amused. 'You haven't answered the question.'

Lee opened her mouth, closed it, then said, 'Definitely not, thank you all the same.'

'In that case, would a marriage of convenience be out of the question?'

She eyed him cautiously.

'Your convenience,' he added pointedly.

Lee swallowed some coffee and looked nervous. 'It could only be supremely inconvenient for you, though,' she suggested.

He shrugged. 'If we both know where we stand, I don't see that it should. In fact, in one aspect it could be quite convenient for me at the moment.'

'What aspect is that?' she asked, feeling a lot like Alice when she had just fallen down the rabbit hole.

'It would suit me to move into Plover Park for a time.'

'*Why?*'

'I'm due for a break, but I also have plans to open a branch office in Byron Bay. I could combine the two and—' he smiled faintly '—keep an eye on my half of the deal at the same time.'

This time Lee knocked over her coffee cup, although fortunately it was empty. Byron Bay was half an hour's drive from Plover Park.

'For the almost ten months left until we're allowed to dispose of Plover Park?' she asked weakly.

He righted her cup and poured her some more coffee. 'No, for as long as it takes. Long enough to quash any doubts that we are at least giving Cyril's dreams for us a go,' he said with a touch of irony.

'I...I don't know what to say.'

'Then let me point out the alternative, Lee. Legal battles which I would not be able to conduct myself since I would be subject to litigation as well as you. Even if we won—and there's a grey area here that could be open to interpretation—it would be a long, uncomfortable road.'

This silenced Lee effectively and she tried to sort it all out in her mind. Then she frowned mightily and spoke—unwisely, as it happened. 'This all seems to dovetail together so well I'm...suspicious!'

Damien lay back in his chair and studied her comprehensively.

Lee fiddled with her scarf and contrived in every way known to her to project unconcern at the scrutiny she was being subjected to. But it was hard going. Because, more than any man she had ever met, Damien Moore was capable of injecting an element of speculation into the way he studied you as a woman, out of those fine dark eyes. Speculation as to what you'd be like in bed, to put it bluntly, she told herself. But it was a curiously disinterested speculation and she hated it!

However, she immediately reminded herself, as she sipped her coffee and tried to look soignée—in spirit if not in grooming—that sadly there was more to the reason she hated it than pure feminine outrage.

There was guilt, for example. Because almost from the moment she'd first met him a certain thought had crossed her mind from time to time—would this dark, clever man, with his wide shoulders, long, strong limbs, his good looks, be dynamite in bed or what?

Guilt also because she was never able to remain unmoved by that speculative study. Even if she managed to hide it, her pulses always started to hammer, mental images of the two of them together plagued her, and it required an almost superhuman effort not to look all hot and bothered.

Then there had been the stage when she'd been sure she'd fallen in love with him, only to have to disabuse herself of the theory—which she had, she assured herself!—because there had never been a glimmer of a similar emotion in him. Sure, he did occasionally look right through her clothes, but only in that speculative way. And how could you go on fancying yourself in love with a man who had proposed a purely platonic marriage?

She grimaced unwittingly. She might try to take a light approach in her thoughts, but underneath there was still a painful little scar to do with Damien Moore. True, the acquisition of Plover Park had helped to take her mind away from him...but now this!

'Suspicious how?' he asked at last.

She looked frustrated. 'I...I don't know. It's just too neat and natty.'

'I am only proposing that we share the same roof, not the same bed, if that's your concern,' he drawled.

She shot him a fiery glance and wondered what he'd do if he knew just why that offended her.

Then she flinched visibly as, almost as if he had read her thoughts, he added, 'Well, not necessarily the same bed—unless you'd like to rethink that bit?'

'No way, José!' were the words that sprang to her lips.

He laughed softly, but said, 'I do admire your pithy turn of phrase, Lee. You never leave anyone in doubt as to your emotions.'

She pinched her lips together, but inwardly breathed a sigh of relief.

'You are also...' he paused, then shrugged '...very refreshing at times.' His dark gaze drifted to the waitress who had simpered over him, and became tinged with irony.

She frowned faintly as she wondered what he was thinking, then shook her head. 'Assuming I agree to this—but there's a very good chance I won't!—when would you want to move in?'

'In about two weeks.'

'So we'd have to...do it...before then.'

'We would have to..."do it"...before then,' he agreed. 'It wouldn't be akin to going to the electric chair, however.'

'I didn't say that.' She gestured helplessly. 'I just…I need a bit of time to think about it!'

'Is there such a lot to think about, Lee?' he asked impatiently. 'Have I not represented your best interests until now?'

She stared at him uncertainly, and it crossed her mind to wonder whether he had any idea what *her* view of her best interests was—not to allow herself to build up dangerous dreams around this man! How much harder would that be if she was married to him, even platonically?

'I…' She stopped.

He looked at his watch and swore beneath his breath—but not, as it turned out, on account of her. 'I'm sorry, you're right. I'm just so damn busy at the moment. I have to go—but do think about it, Lee.'

'It's not as if there isn't enough room,' she said, then looked shocked.

He grinned. 'At Plover Park? True. But never let it be said I rushed you into anything.' He stood up. 'Look, I'm sorry, but I *really* have to go. Why don't you order something more to your taste? I'll leave an imprint of my credit card with them. Please let me know your decision in due course,' he added formally.

Lee stared up at him. 'OK. Bye!'

He hesitated for a moment, then, 'Don't do anything I wouldn't, Lee Westwood. Goodbye.' He turned away.

She watched his retreating back. It would be fair to say, she thought darkly, that he cut a swathe through the female population of the café—and the waitress he had eyed earlier tripped over her feet in her eagerness to be the one to deal with his bill.

It would also be fair to say he had it all: an aura of power and wealth, a hint of arrogance, a touch of damning uninterest in the ripples he was creating in many a womanly heart. But it was, curiously, no consolation, she brooded, to know that she was not alone in finding Damien Moore irresistible.

She reached for her coffee cup, then jumped as a voice beside her said, 'Having lunch with him now and then is not going to do it, you know.' And a man slid into the seat Damien had vacated.

'Who on earth are you and what do you mean?' she asked haughtily.

'And good day to you too, Miss Westwood,' he returned. 'I happen to be Cyril Delaney's brother—Cosmo.'

'What?' Lee's eyes nearly popped out on stalks, then she realised there was a definite resemblance, although this man's blue eyes were unpleasantly shifty and knowing. 'You're the one who's contesting the will?'

'The same,' he agreed.

She gasped. 'Are you having me followed? Is that why you're here?'

'Not at all,' he denied. 'This is pure coincidence. I recognised Damien Moore and put two and two together. I also thought it might be a timely opportunity to make it known to you that I intend to fight the bequest my brother was conned into making to you and Moore every inch of the way.' He bared his teeth unpleasantly.

'Conned! You're out of your mind!'

'Am I? He promised me Plover Park, so as I see it, between the two of you, you must have pitched him some kind of a con to get the place out of him. I certainly see no evidence that you two are the loving couple he hoped you would be!'

Lee stood up and said dramatically, 'Do your best, Cosmo Delaney. Or should I say your worst?' And she stalked away.

She was halfway to her car when she began to calm down and think more rationally. Then she fumbled for her mobile phone in her string bag and punched in the number of Moore & Moore. But it took a frustrating five minutes of dealing with receptionists and an over-zealous secretary before she got Damien.

He said coolly, 'This had better be good, Lee.'

She made a frustrated sound in her throat. 'It is! I need to talk to you!'

'I can't talk now, I'm in a conference. If it's that urgent we'll have to meet after work. Damn,' he added immediately, 'I've been invited to a party tonight, and I'm going to have to work late anyway, so—'

'Excellent!' Lee broke in. 'I'll come to the party with you—if you're not taking someone else?'

There was dead silence down the line, then, 'I beg your pardon?'

'I said I'll come with you if—*are* you taking someone else?'

'No, but...'

'Could this party stand an extra guest at short notice?' she queried.

'Uh...well it's not a sit-down dinner, it's an *al fresco* buffet with dancing, so—'

'Even better!' Lee pronounced. 'Sounds like my kind of party. The only thing is I need somewhere to park myself in the meantime. Any chance of using your apartment?'

Another silence.

'Damien?'

'You want to get into my apartment?'

'It beats pounding pavements all afternoon. Besides, I need somewhere to get into my party gear.'

'I—'

'Damien, if you don't let me do this I'll come and picket your office,' she warned. 'This *is* urgent.'

'All right. I'll phone the building manager and tell him to let you in. Uh—do you have party gear with you?'

She thought there was a certain amount of caution with which he asked this, and smiled to herself. 'No. But I have a credit card—and I'll endeavour not to embarrass you.'

*   *   *

The beautician in the department store beauty salon was talkative as she did Lee's nails and gave her a mini-facial. She was also drop-dead gorgeous, with inch-long fake eyelashes and a streak of pink through her hair. She went by the name of Sally.

'Got to be a guy involved?' she hazarded. 'Planning on doing a Cinderella?'

Lee grimaced mentally; she was unable to do so physically because of the mask on her face. 'You could say so,' she mumbled. 'I know I look a bit strange to be in a beauty parlour.'

Sally shrugged. 'I take it he's quite some guy?'

'Well, yes,' Lee confessed. 'He's one of those dark, damn you kind of men. I mean, he's all proper and correct most of the time, but you get the feeling that underneath he could be quite different.'

'The kind to drive women wild?' Sally suggested.

'Exactly. I must be mad,' Lee added.

'No. I always say go for it. Give 'em a bit of their own medicine. You only live once, you're only young once, and you sure have the hair and the eyes to do it.'

'Thanks, but I thought there was more to it.'

Sally glanced down the length of Lee. 'They say you can never be too rich or too thin.'

This time Lee had to laugh, and cracked the mask.

'Never mind, it's ready to come off. Have you got a dress in mind?' Sally enquired.

'That's next on my agenda.'

'Go for black, and go mini, so you can dazzle him with your legs—there's a dress right here in this store that would be divine on you. I'm due for a break when I finish you— like me to show you it? I'd almost set my heart on it myself, but I can tell this is a worthy cause so I'll pass.'

'That's—I don't know whether to laugh or cry, but that's very noble of you!'

'Wait until you see yourself in it,' Sally advised. 'Might

just change your mind about yourself. And it might just get him grovelling.'

An hour later, Lee emerged from a cubicle in the dress department of the store and examined herself in the mirror from all angles.

'What did I tell you?' Sally said, at the slightly stunned look in Lee's eyes.

'You don't think it's too—?'

'No way! Go to it, honey! But I'd put your hair up.'

A couple of hours later she was being ushered into a luxury high-rise apartment at Kangaroo Point, with sweeping views of the Brisbane River and the city centre on the opposite bank.

She thanked the building manager, and as he left dropped several elegant shopping bags onto a claret-coloured settee.

She'd only been in his apartment once before, when he'd asked her to breakfast, but it was equally as impressive today. Acres of off-white carpet, lovely paintings and *objets d'art*, with touches of hyacinth-pink and blue to complement the claret in the soft furnishings. There was even a bowl of fresh creamy pink carnations on the coffee table.

She looked at her watch and discovered she still had a few hours to kill. Time enough to relax for a bit, so she wandered into the den, turned the television on and lay down on the broad leather couch to watch a movie. In fact, she fell asleep, and it was dark when she woke, although she still had over an hour to prepare herself for the party.

Then she realised her tummy was rumbling so she raided her lawyer's kitchen, which proved to be a fairly barren experience, but she did find some cheese and crackers, an apple and some grapes. Damien obviously rarely ate at home, although she did notice several bottles of champagne in the fridge. Then she went to look for the spare bedroom. On the way to it she passed the main bedroom, and it crossed her mind to wonder whether her future husband-in-name-only entertained any lovers in it.

She hesitated at the doorway. Common sense told her that Damien would not live like a monk, and ethics persuaded her she should not snoop, so she bypassed the room resolutely. But that spark of curiosity remained.

The spare bedroom had its own *en-suite* bathroom, she discovered, and, paradoxically, it held all the answers her spark of curiosity cried out to know. Not only was there a full set of a famous brand of luxury cosmetics set out on the marble vanity stand, but there was a robe and matching nightgown hanging from a hook on the wall. A very sensuous robe and nightgown, at that, being fashioned of sheer coffee silk with fine ecru lace inserts.

She raised her eyebrows and tried to picture the girl who owned these telltale items. Tall, she found as she measured the robe against herself. Taller than her five feet four, and a glance at the size on the label told her that this girl was more generously curved, for it was a size larger than the size she took. So, tall and shapely, she decided. Dark or fair? She picked up the brush on the vanity and discovered a couple of long dark strands of hair in it. Definitely a brunette, then. She picked up a tube of lipstick, a deep berry-red, and found a bottle of nail polish that matched it.

OK, she got the picture, she mused. Tall, dark and dramatically attractive—that went without saying when you thought of Damien's good looks. Not your shrinking violet kind of girl either. Possibly a career girl? Possibly another lawyer?

Then it occurred to her that there might be clothes in the closet owned by this girl—and indeed there were. Not many, but enough to confirm her impressions that this girl was striking and probably a professional career woman. For despite their lovely colours they were severely tailored and very formal.

She looked down at her jeans and boots with a grimace,

but then remembered her shopping bags and ran through to the lounge to retrieve them.

The dress she'd bought was uncrushable, which was fortunate because she'd forgotten to hang it up. And as she carried it through to the spare bedroom, along with the shoes, make-up and underwear she'd purchased, she decided that in this dress there was no reason for her not to give any number of striking, professional women a run for their money—despite her chosen career being that of a landscape gardener.

She paused at the thought of her career and swallowed suddenly as Cosmo Delaney swam into her mind's eye. The surprise acquisition of Plover Park *had* provided her with the means not only to help her grandparents but also to make the dream of a lifetime start to come true. She and her grandfather had not only been able to maintain the nursery so that a good income was coming in, but she'd also received two commissions to design gardens. She closed her eyes at the thought of losing it all, and reminded herself that was why she was here in Damien Moore's apartment.

But that posed a question. Was she really prepared to marry Damien Moore to hang on to Cyril Delaney's bequest?

She sank down on to the bed with her dress in her arms. And where did this tall, dark, striking woman who stored her clothes in his spare bedroom fit in with his proposal to move to Plover Park?

An hour later, she was ready.

Her hair, on Sally's advice, was up in an elegant twist. The dress fitted like a glove. Her lips were painted to match her nails, and all in all it was a startling metamorphosis from the girl who had sat down to lunch with Damien Moore earlier in the day. She wondered, with a tinge of acerbity, what he would make of her transformation.

She only had to wait a few minutes before his key turned in the lock...

CHAPTER THREE

'HOLY...mackerel!'

About half the width of the lamplit lounge separated them when Damien Moore stopped as if shot and made his observation at the same time.

Lee's lips trembled but she managed to say gravely, 'On the pithy sayings scale that's nearly as good as...no way, José! Not what you'd expect of a legal brain, mind, but very expressive. Not that complimentary either—but I gather I've surprised you?'

He took in the little black dress she wore and blinked. What there was of it hugged her figure. The bodice was heart-shaped, revealing a tantalising glimpse of her décolleté, and was held up by narrow straps encrusted with rhinestones. The skirt stopped well above her knees. High black patent sandals adorned her narrow feet and her legs were bare.

It was a dress her slender figure and her lightly tanned limbs did justice to. It was a dress that revealed a more tantalising figure than he had suspected, and against the black her green eyes were stunning, her freckles almost unnoticeable. Her very light make-up was perfect as well. In all aspects *she* could suddenly have stepped out of the pages of *Vogue*...

He spoke at last. 'It is a bit different from your everlasting jeans, boots and odd scarves—and, of course, your black hat.'

'I'm a gardener, remember? It needs to be a very special occasion for me to dress up. Would it be too much to ask if you approve?'

'Would you care if I didn't?' he countered, and strolled forward, then started to circle her slowly.

'No.' She said it a shade sharply, because of course she would, but she'd rather die than allow him to see it. Nor did she appreciate being inspected as if she were a prize filly. It made her wonder if he'd pick up her feet and check her teeth. Not only that, it set her nerve-ends tingling and caused her to feel that she might as well not have bothered to clothe herself at all.

'In the context of your party,' she rephrased tartly, 'it'd be nice to know if I come up to scratch.'

He came round to stand in front of her and a fleeting smile touched his mouth. 'I think you look sensational, Miss Westwood. In any context. There's also more to you than your clothes have hitherto led me to suspect, and I apologise for my tactless remark at lunch.'

She bit her lip and tried not to colour as his dark gaze roamed over her exposed flesh—and there was quite a lot of it. She realised, too late, that his reference to her figure at lunch must have lingered in her subconscious and been the reason she'd allowed herself to be persuaded into this dress. A subliminal desire to prove a thing or two to him, to be precise. She might be slim but she wasn't scrawny. Only to have him see right through her...

She said, after a moment's intense thought, 'I'm very pleased to hear it, Damien, but I asked that in a *particular* context—I need to make a statement! I need to stand out from the crowd tonight. I need to be noticed as your...' She hesitated, then bit the bullet, 'As your prospective wife.'

'There's little doubt you'll be noticed,' he said wryly, 'but why this sudden change of heart?'

She brought him up to date. 'I know you told me most of this, but coming face to face with Cosmo Delaney and hearing him say that Cyril had promised Plover Park to him really brought it home, I guess,' she finished.

He pulled off his jacket and tie and slung them over the back of a chair. 'I see.'

'He...he gives me the creeps—Cosmo Delaney,' she added with a shudder.

'Do you think he overheard our conversation?'

Lee considered. 'No. If he'd been that close I'm sure I'd have got the vibes.' She frowned. 'You don't seem at all perturbed.'

Damien shrugged. 'I spend my life dealing with this kind of thing. I've also had a long, busy day.' He touched a cupboard and a door sprang open to reveal the lit interior of a cocktail cabinet. 'Like a drink?'

'No, thanks. Of course,' she said arctically, and looked around the luxury apartment, 'being wealthy in your own right obviously gives you a different perspective on all this. It doesn't mean nearly as much to you as it does to me. It probably doesn't mean anything to you at all!' Her green eyes were accusing.

He poured himself a Scotch and soda and took it over to the settee. 'On the contrary, Lee,' he murmured as he sprawled back, stretched his long legs out and looked up at her lazily. 'If anyone could prove I conned myself into Cyril's will under false pretences, I could kiss my career goodbye.'

She stared at him, then sank into an armchair. 'Why aren't you more upset, then?'

He studied his glass. 'Before I go into that perhaps I should make a point. The easiest course for me at this stage, Lee, would be to withdraw any claim on Plover Park.'

Her lips parted and her eyes widened.

'I don't need the place,' he continued wryly. 'I don't need the hassle of all this. And, although I don't intend to do it, perhaps you should bear it in mind.'

She sprang up, then with a frustrated little sound crossed to the cocktail cabinet and mixed herself a brandy and soda—a process Damien watched with amusement. 'I'm speechless,' she remarked as she returned to her chair beneath his gaze.

'Good. Perhaps you'll hear me out in silence, then. The reason I'm not going to do it is this. For whatever reason...' He paused and looked into the distance with a tinge of irony in his eyes. 'I admired your fight for your grandparents. Nor *did* I in any way pressure Cyril into putting us in his will. He also left Cosmo a significant inheritance in other forms. So I'll continue the fight.'

'That's all?' she said uncertainly.

'No.' He stood up and looked down at her quizzically. 'While I may continue the fight, the histrionics are your department, not mine.'

Lee bit her lip.

He smiled faintly, then said abruptly, 'Are you quite sure you want to do this?'

'A…marriage in name only,' she said, 'for the next ten months?'

'Precisely, Lee. I have no deep, dark intentions towards you, believe me.' He said it a shade grimly.

She pressed her hands together and took a very deep breath. 'Yes, I'm sure.'

'All right. Hang on a moment.'

He left the room and came back shortly with a small velvet box which he handed to her. 'It's just occurred to me that we might as well use tonight to announce our engagement—after a whirlwind romance.'

Lee's startled gaze rested on him, then flicked down to the box.

'Open it.'

She did. To find a small but exceptionally pure diamond ring in an antique setting. Her mouth fell open and her gaze flew back to his. 'What's this?'

'What it looks like. An engagement ring,' he said dryly.

'But…how come you just happen to have an engagement ring on hand? I mean—'

'I've had it for years,' he interrupted. 'An aunt of mine left me all her possessions in *her* will, that's all. Try it on.'

For an insane moment she was tempted to say…*You should be doing this*. Then she swallowed and asked herself if she were mad. She put the ring on the third finger of her left hand. It fitted well. 'It's…very nice,' she said.

He studied it on her slender hand, but made no comment other than to excuse himself to take a shower and change.

It took him fifteen minutes, and when he reappeared he wore a fawn linen jacket, white open-necked shirt and khaki gabardine trousers. He looked casual yet complete, and as if he could go anywhere. His dark hair was sleek and still damp. He'd also retrieved a bottle of French champagne from the fridge in the kitchen.

'Ready?'

Lee stood up and smoothed her dress down nervously. 'How far do we have to go?'

He frowned faintly and studied her oval face beneath the heavy, beautifully upswept hair. 'Only upstairs. My friends own the penthouse. There's a vast terrace up there and the view's great—what's wrong?'

'Serious butterflies in my stomach, if you really want to know.' She smiled palely.

'Don't you go to parties?'

'Of course! Well, not a lot these days—and not generally on penthouse terraces with million-dollar views—but that's not the problem.'

'I thought I'd reassured you that you do look the part?' His dark gaze swept up and down her.

'Thanks.'

'What is the problem, then? I got the distinct impression you could handle yourself in any circumstances and didn't give a damn what anyone thought of you.' He looked wry. 'My one-woman SWAT team fiancée.'

'Thank you,' she said sardonically. 'I *can* handle myself. I—damn,' she said and closed her eyes briefly. 'It's just that I have no idea how to pretend I'm your fiancée!'

'Ah. Where's the movie star attitude?'

'This is *different* from walking into a restaurant.'

'And you're trying to tell me you hadn't thought of that bit when you gave me no choice but to take you to this party?'

'Damien—yes,' she admitted hollowly. 'I just…Cosmo unsettled me and—'

'Made you rush in where angels fear to tread?' he supplied. 'You have to admit, Lee, it's not the first time it's happened to you.'

A confrontational glint lit her eyes. 'OK, we both know I can be rash and all the rest, but *you* were the one who first brought this… spirit-of-the-bequest to life for me—so do you have any suggestions?'

He put the champagne down on the coffee table next to the carnations and shoved his hands into his pockets. 'Well,' he mused, 'it's to be expected we are fairly besotted with each other. So, if you really want to make a statement tonight, you have between here and the penthouse to polish up your besotted act.'

She gazed at him fiercely. 'If you think it's funny, Damien Moore, I don't!'

'I do, I'm afraid. Where's your sense of humour, Lee?'

'It's taking a break. Look—' she sat down suddenly '—I don't think I can do this. You go.'

'What will that show Cosmo Delaney?' he enquired.

She clenched her fists but said, 'It's not as if he'll be there—or will he?' Her eyes widened.

He shook his head. 'Not a chance. We could find ourselves in the society pages of the Sunday papers, however.'

Lee suffered a sudden vision of her nursery. The hundreds of callistemons or bottlebrush, for example. She had rescued them from near death by neglect and was now set to make a nice profit on them. The rows upon rows of fledgling melaleucas or paper bark she was growing. The lillypilly shrubs she found invaluable in garden design, for their bright green shiny leaves, colourful berries and the way their spring growth was often a startling pink.

She had a nursery full of these native shrubs that were so popular because they attracted native birds: lorikeets, rosellas, parrots in all their colourful splendour. She had many more as well, and she'd just received a commission to design the garden of a luxury home at Lennox Head.

She opened her mouth, closed it, and stood up cautiously. 'We'd have to get our stories right...'

'Undoubtedly,' he agreed, and she could have killed him because he was still amused.

In fact so telling was the look she shot him that he laughed softly, then sobered. 'How about this? We met when you approached me for legal advice and it all flowed on from there. Keep it as simple as that. Oh, and don't worry about the besotted bit.'

'Why?' she asked uncertainly.

He looked down at her with a wicked glint in his eyes. Then he took a perfect creamy carnation from the bowl beside the champagne, snapped it off so there was only a couple of inches of stem left, and tucked the flower between her breasts. 'I'll take care of it.'

'Damien, you dark horse!'

Ella Patroni, hostess extraordinaire—even Lee recognised her from reports of her famous parties, charity endeavours and spending sprees—looked genuinely stunned on being presented with Damien's fiancée. But she recovered in a flash and Lee found herself being all but smothered in a flurry of amber shot-silk caftan—Ella's voluminous attire—as she was hugged enthusiastically.

'You clever kid,' Ella said. 'There've been many who've tried to nail him to the altar but none of them thought of doing it secretly. I'll bet that's why you succeeded!'

Damien raised an eyebrow at this monumentally tactless observation but said nothing. And Lee, trying to appear nonchalant but still suffering from the feel of his fingers between her breasts, looked beyond their hostess to a vista that made her eyes widen and made her temporarily forget the embarrassment of her situation.

Through the huge sliding glass doors the penthouse terrace resembled a tropical island. There were palm trees, a thatched hut that served as a bar, burning braziers and fairy lights, and a lit pool. The lack of sand and sea was a detail that didn't seem to detract from the overall scene at all, and, to her amazement and amusement, the waiters and waitresses attending to the lively colourful throng of guests were dressed up as characters out of *Gilligan's Island*.

There was a Ginger in gold lamé and a Mary Ann in bunches and gingham, circulating with trays of champagne. The Professor was behind the bar mixing cocktails and the Skipper was helping him. Mr and Mrs Howell, impeccably and authentically attired, were offering hors d'oeuvres. Only Gilligan was not waiting upon guests. He was tinkling at the ivories of a white piano that stood in a small replica of the *Minnow*, draped with a fishing net and colourful starfish.

'That's wonderful!' Lee said, and turned a laughing face back to Ella.

'Mmm…mmm!' Ella put her head to one side. 'I bet it was those eyes that got you in, Damien. They are quite stunning! OK, how do you want to handle this? Save a lot of time and effort if we just announce it, don't you think?'

'No…'

'Yes…'

Lee and Damien spoke together, she in the negative.

'Lee,' he said patiently, 'let's get it over and done with.'

'I—'

'He's got a point,' Ella put in. 'I mean if word spreads slowly you'll have people coming up to you all night asking if it's true. Trust me, pet, I'll do it myself. Come with me.' She took Lee's hand and surged out on to the terrace.

In the last moments before the world and its wife became aware that she was about to marry Damien Moore, Lee was prey to a sinking sensation that told her she might not have given it enough thought. She was familiar with this sensation. She did often act on impulse, but she was generally able to damn the consequences on the basis that her intentions were always of the best. This time she wasn't so sure. Not about her motives but about the consequences…

Then, as Ella commandeered the microphone and 'Gilligan' played the piano equivalent of a drum roll, Damien took her hand and raised it to his lips. 'Don't look as if you're going to the gallows, Lee,' he murmured so only she could hear. 'It spoils the effect.'

She swallowed, and was electrified because he then dispensed with her hand and drew her into his arms as Ella proclaimed through the microphone, 'Friends, Romans and countrymen, I give you Damien Moore and his fiancée Lee Westwood!'

A dramatic hush fell over the party, then an excited babble broke out while Damien kissed her leisurely and for the first time.

'Oh!' she said as they broke apart. Gilligan started to play 'Here Comes the Bride'...and they were besieged by well-wishers.

He observed her flushed cheeks and stunned eyes. 'Not very pithy, Miss Westwood,' he said softly. 'Could I have surprised you?'

There was no chance to answer him—not that she'd come up with anything pithy in the meantime—because she was being introduced left, right and centre to his friends.

Why the secrecy? was the most common comment.

To Lee's surprise—although it shouldn't have come as a surprise, she mused darkly—Damien fielded the comment every time with suave ease and a stroke of genius. He intimated to all and sundry, not only by what he said but by the way he looked at her, that he'd wanted to keep her to himself for a while.

She even saw several women close their eyes and sigh soulfully at the way his dark gaze lingered on her, full of sensual appreciation and ownership.

Come to that, she herself was having trouble with that sensual appreciation and ownership, and it caused her to stumble a couple of times on the way to the dance floor as the buzz subsided and the party got back to normal.

'Wasn't too bad, was it?'

She bit her lip. 'No.'

'Once again, you don't sound too sure,' he remarked wryly.

'I just get the feeling you're…too good at this.'

He raised an eyebrow.

'Too practised is what I mean.' She frowned. 'As if you could do it for a living.'

'That's a serious charge to lay, Lee,' he replied seriously but something at the back of his eyes was laughing at her.

'Well,' she soldiered on, 'it can't be for real, but it rolled off you as if it were.'

He grinned openly. 'I am thirty-six, so I guess a bit of practice has come my way. I also believe if you're going to do something you might as well do it properly.' He swung her to the music and pulled her back into his arms.

It was extremely hard, she discovered, to maintain a severe stance this close to Damien Moore. He danced well, better than she was managing to do beneath the weight of everything that had happened to her tonight—and he'd obviously assessed that, so he was keeping it simple and providing her with plenty of lead. Plenty of opportunity also, she reflected darkly, to come into contact with a fair proportion of his tall, lean and streamlined body.

There was also that dark gaze of his to deal with, and the way it rested on the lowest point of her heart-shaped bodice where her skin was pearl pale and the swell of her breast visible. She'd removed the carnation in the lift and tucked it into her hair, but she now regretted it. Because every time he glanced down at her his gaze lingered there for a moment and it was as if his fingers were brushing her nipples and spreading ripples of sensuous delight through her. It was impossible to maintain a steady rate of breathing beneath this onslaught, and once again she tripped.

Whereupon, like a lover, he gathered her close and kissed the top of her head. Close enough for Lee to be struck by a new knowledge of Damien Moore. Until tonight his attraction had mostly been in his aura. Now she could feel the muscle beneath his clothes, the slip and flow of a strong, athletic body as he moved her effortlessly through the rhythm of the music. She was close enough to be fascinated by the feel of him, and all her senses were crying out for her to melt against him...

It was no consolation either that she'd always suspected he would have this effect on her. She'd had a fair intimation of it, even although until now the closest physical contact they'd had was a handshake and his hand on her arm. And the reason it was no consolation—or one of the reasons— was the visible effect he had on most women.

Very humiliating to join a queue, she brooded. How much more humiliating to know that for him it was all an act?

'You were saying?' He broke in on her bittersweet reflections as the music stopped.

She blinked. 'Did I say something?'

He stopped dancing and held her loosely around her waist. 'No. But your thought processes were almost written on your forehead.' He scanned her flushed face and the way tendrils of auburn hair clung to her neck. 'It was obvious you were conducting an internal conversation.'

'I've had a lot surprises today, one way or another,' she returned with dignity. 'It's only surprising I'm not talking aloud to myself.'

He laughed and dropped a light kiss—on her forehead this time.

She flinched inwardly, and to cover it said, 'By the way, the state of your larder leaves a lot to be desired.'

He looked surprised, then comprehending. 'Didn't you order another lunch?'

'No. Cosmo managed to destroy what little of my appetite was left after you broke your news.'

'Let's eat, then.' He released her and took her hand. 'I think this is the dinner break anyway. I just hope there is something to suit your specialised tastes.'

* * *

There was, and they took their laden plates to an unoccupied table amongst the colourful, noisy throng.

Lee had chosen seafood: delicious prawns, smoked salmon and salad.

'Don't you ever eat any meat?' Damien enquired.

'No. I don't eat a lot of meat—and you shouldn't ask those kinds of questions in public. It could spoil the effect.'

He looked around. 'I stand corrected.' He ordered a bottle of wine from 'Thurston Howell the Third.'

'Tell me something.' Lee gazed across at Ella, sitting nearby surrounded by people. 'Is there a Mr Patroni?'

'Yes. He goes by the name of Hank and he'll be here somewhere. He's not as flamboyant as Ella.'

'Concentrates on making the money while Ella concentrates on spending it?'

'Something like that,' Damien agreed wryly. 'By the way, I've had a thought. I assume you intend to spend the night here?' He glanced at her.

Lee toyed with a prawn. This was something else she hadn't given the proper amount of thought to, but unless she cared to embark on a three-hour drive in the middle of the night what was her alternative? 'I might,' she said carefully.

He lowered his voice and said with irony, 'You're welcome to the spare bedroom.'

'How kind of you,' she replied *sotto voce*, although what she would have liked to ask was—did he have any idea how his spare bedroom reinforced just what a farce all this was?

'Good,' he commented. 'Then, as tomorrow is a Saturday, I can take you to meet my mother.'

Lee dropped her fork. He courteously retrieved it, handed it over to the Skipper, and requested a clean one.

Anything she wanted to say on the subject of meeting his mother was forestalled as a man came up to them and introduced himself as Hank Patroni. He also had a plate in his hand and he sat down with them.

An hour later the music struck up again, reinforced by a disco this time. During the hour Lee had not only made the acquaintance of Hank Patroni, but several more of Damien's closer friends. People who might rightfully be consumed by a burning curiosity on the subject of Damien's forthcoming marriage but were too polite to probe directly. All the same their curiosity was palpable, and for Lee it was like walking on eggshells.

She had no idea, for example, that her future husband was a scratch golfer and held a helicopter pilot's licence. She was unaware that he had a sister, Melinda. She didn't know that his mother was a Family Court judge, although on discovering this she swore to herself to avoid the woman at all costs. And she nearly fell off her chair to find out that Damien part-owned the horse that had won the last Melbourne Cup.

In fact, it was under the weight of all this new knowledge, and the strain of pretending to be abreast of it, that she took herself off to the powder room to regroup as best she could.

Ella personally showed her into her own bedroom and the *en-suite* bathroom. 'Take your time, pet,' she advised. 'I'm sure this has been a big night for you!'

No flies on Ella Patroni, Lee mused, as she was left alone. She stared at herself in the mirror, in a sea of black marble tiling and gold fittings, and laid her small evening purse on the vanity stand. Even she could see the slightly stunned look in her green eyes.

She looked around and discovered that this bathroom had what appeared to be a foot bath set into the floor, with a low, elegant gold chair placed beside it. Ella seemed to live a pampered lifestyle. It made sense that she liked to bathe her feet from time to time. It occurred to Lee she would like nothing better than to bathe her own feet—although it didn't seem a particularly guest-like pursuit. She hesitated, then sat down, pulled her new shoes off and ran cold water over her feet into the bath. At the press of a button the bath became a miniature spa. She sat back with a sigh of sheer pleasure.

She would never be unkind about Ella's extravagance again, she decided. This woman knew how to live, and because of her she, Lee Westwood, might just be able to go back to the party and cope.

She should have known, though, she reflected, that there was an awful lot of substance behind Damien Moore. She'd ridden in the Porsche he drove; she'd seen his apartment; she'd had to fight tooth and nail to get an appointment with him in the first place. And she'd only fought for that appointment, she recalled, because her research into law firms and their successes had led her to believe he was the one man who might be able to take Cyril Delaney on. Why then, she pondered, should it surprise her that everything else he touched turned to gold?

'I'll tell you what is really surprising, Lee,' she said to herself—and didn't give a damn that she had actually reached the stage where she was talking to herself out loud. 'It doesn't make sense that this prince among men should marry you when he barely knows you just because of a bequest in a will that is probably very small potatoes to him anyway!'

'OK?'

'Fine, thank you,' Lee replied brightly to her fiancé.

He took in her freshly applied make-up, the sheen of her lips, her tidied hair, her generally cool appearance and fragrant perfume—and the certain glint in her eye which caused him to narrow his own. He knew that look. It generally meant Lee was on her mettle. 'You took so long I was beginning to wonder if you'd done a bunk.'

'I was bathing my feet.'

His eyebrows shot up.

'I know,' she agreed with a grin, 'but Ella has this dinky little foot bath of which I availed myself at the same time as I regrouped.'

He looked down at her feet, then up into her eyes. 'Let's see if I've got this right—you needed to bathe your feet in order to regroup?'

'You should try it, Damien, it's delicious!'

'Why, may I enquire, did you need to regroup?'

She shrugged. 'It's an exhausting let alone dicey game we're playing—more so for me, of course. There's not much you don't know about me. There's not an awful lot *to* know about me, come to that,' she added candidly. 'Although—' she cocked her ear to the beat of the disco '—there is one thing.'

'I've got the feeling I'm going to regret this, but what is that?'

She favoured him with a sparkling look of mischief. 'I may not have been much fun to push around the dance floor earlier, but this could be another matter.'

'Show me,' he said slowly.

'All right. No hands, though,' she warned. 'I like to do my own thing to this beat.'

'I knew I was going to regret this,' he replied humorously, 'but if that's what you want, no hands.'

It wasn't until nearly an hour later that he broke his word. But Lee took no exception to it. She collapsed into his arms, having danced herself to a standstill. In fact they'd become the cynosure of all eyes, because if she was an innovative and spirited disco dancer, so was he. There was even applause when they stopped.

'What did you put into that foot bath?' he asked wryly.

'Whatever it was, it's worn off,' she responded breathlessly. 'Take me home, please.'

'With pleasure,' he replied, hugging her and kissing her lightly—to more enthusiastic applause. As they left the floor 'Gilligan' played the traditional bridal farewell, the guests formed a guard of honour with Ella and Hank at the head of it—and that was how they left the party.

'I've never been to a party like that!'

Lee stood in the middle of Damien's lounge and slipped off her shoes. Damien put a glass of champagne into her hand. She looked at the bubbles inside the frosted glass, then sipped—it was delicious.

'You were inspired,' he murmured. 'You made your statement loud and clear.'

'Only because something you said stuck with me,' she said slowly, before the realisation that she might have made more of a statement than she'd intended to hit her.

He looked at her enquiringly.

'If you're going to do something you might as well do it properly.'

He considered this, eyeing her slim figure in the lovely dress, the damp tendrils of her hair clinging to her skin, the vulnerability of that slender neck. 'On the other hand, I got the impression something put you on your mettle.'

She looked up at him, startled. 'How?'

His lips twisted. 'I've had a bit of experience of you on your mettle, Lee.'

She shrugged and sipped some more champagne. 'I…did feel a bit like Cinderella at one stage,' she conceded gruffly. 'I mean, I could see people wondering what I had that would measure up to…all the things you are.'

'Such as?'

'Damien, surely I don't have to tell you that there is not a lot of substance to me. I don't play golf, I don't drive a Porsche, I don't own Melbourne Cup winners, my mother is not a Family Court judge—and incidentally, on the subject of visiting your mother tomorrow, my answer is no.'

'Leaving that aside for the moment,' he said ruefully, 'most of my friends wouldn't give a damn about your substance, or lack of it, in those areas. Your personality and whether we're in love would be the criteria they'd apply.'

She sank down suddenly into an arm chair. 'But we're not.'

He was silent for a long moment. 'Have you ever been in love?'

She finished her champagne. 'I don't think so. Been through the motions a couple of times, but my considered opinion is there's an awful lot of peer pressure, as well as advertising pressure et cetera—' she tipped her hand '—and that is responsible for flawing one's judgement in these matters.'

He smiled faintly. 'You sound as if you could be a lawyer yourself. And you have a point.'

'Thanks. What about you?'

'I've...also been through the motions a few times.' He looked amused. 'To date, nothing has come to fruition.'

She glanced at him through her lashes and bit her tongue on the question she longed to ask. Where was the dark-haired beauty he was going through the motions with at the moment?

'As for visiting my mother tomorrow,' he said, 'I—'

She stood up and broke in determinedly. 'Damien, I'm exhausted. Would you mind if I crashed on your couch in the den?'

He looked her over impassively. 'What's wrong with the spare room?'

'I...I...I'd be happier in the den—'

'Lee, there is no chance of me taking advantage of you in the spare room. Come to that it would be just as easy to do it in the den, were I so minded.'

She stuck her chin out. 'It's not that. I may be exhausted, but sometimes I suffer from insomnia—I could watch television, very quietly so as not to disturb you, of course, if that happens tonight.'

He studied her narrowly.

'You see,' she ploughed on, 'for quite a few years, I lived in a bedsit—the couch was a convertible bed, if you know what I mean—so I...got used to sleeping in front of the television.'

'Why are you babbling, Lee?'

She blushed. 'I'm really tired. And I don't want to go and see your mother tomorrow!'

'All right, we'll talk about that in the morning. And you may sleep where you like. I'll get you a blanket and a pillow if it's to be the couch. Do you have anything to sleep in?'

'Uh, well, no...'

'Stay here. I'll get you something.'

She flinched inwardly, but what he brought was a plain white T-shirt of his—not the coffee silk negligée—as well as a blanket and a pillow.

'Thank you,' she said humbly. 'I'm sorry to be so much trouble.'

He put the T-shirt into her hands and tilted her chin. 'You're a strange girl,' he commented. 'I'd sometimes give quids to know what goes on behind those stunning eyes of yours.'

Her lips parted and she stared up at him, caught and drowning in a sudden attack of the mesmerising power Damien Moore could wield over her when he chose. Until today, she thought dazedly, it had happened to her with no physical contact between them. Until today she'd been able to hide the effect it had on her. Tonight, though, physical proximity had made it much more potent.

She'd seen another side of him. A charming, playful side of him that had made his company almost—irresistible. And now, tired and wrung out, she could think of nothing nicer than to melt into his arms and be taken to bed to enjoy anything he might like to institute between them…

She closed her eyes and felt his long fingers drift to the nape of her neck, to stroke it beneath the tendrils of hair that had come down. The effect was unique. Soothing but at the same time arousing, causing her to wonder how you could feel tired but very sexy at the same time. Because there was no doubt she was feeling sexy. There was no doubt something as simple and in no way exceptionally intimate as his fingers on her neck was causing a flurry of activity within.

Delicious tremors were running through her—tremors of anticipation that were directly linked to the thought of being more intimate with Damien Moore. The anticipation of the feel of his hands on her breasts, for example; the anticipation of being held hard against that superbly streamlined body; the anticipation of being made love to by a man she found fascinating even if she was one in a long line of women to do so.

Her lashes lifted to see an unmistakable question in his dark eyes. For a moment she was truly tempted to say, *Yes, do whatever you want, Damien. Make love to me, make me laugh, cry a little, even sing, because I know in my bones that's exactly how you would do it...*

She swallowed and sighed. Talk about the path to destruction! 'I'll go to bed now,' was what she said.

His lips twisted and something—could it have been a brief glint of admiration?—lit his eyes. It was gone before she could be sure.

'All right, Cinderella,' he said wickedly, and kissed her lips. 'Sleep tight.'

Predictably, she didn't sleep well, although she did fall into a deep slumber as the sun rose.

Less predictably, at ten o'clock that Saturday morning she was to be found seated beside him in the Porsche, mutely mutinous, as they drove to his mother's house.

CHAPTER FOUR

'SULKING doesn't become you, Lee.'

Damien flicked the gear lever and they powered off from a traffic light in his metallic blue Porsche.

She said, not turning her head, 'Being a bully doesn't become *you*, Damien.'

He glanced at her, noted that her profile was carved in stone, and smiled absently.

It was also a delicate profile, he found himself thinking, and—possibly because she was still pale with anger—her freckles were more noticeable this morning. Her hair was loose, and it occurred to him that she took less trouble with her hair than any woman he knew. Sometimes she pulled it back into a ponytail, sometimes she pinned it up; mostly she left it to its own devices. She never appeared to be at all frustrated by it.

Could that be because—as she'd demonstrated this morning, when he'd finally woken her—even as she sat up like a sleepy owl her hair looked wonderful? he mused.

She was also wearing her new dress and shoes—another cause of dissent between them.

Then she turned to him abruptly, obviously unable to contain her emotions a second longer. 'What will we tell her?' she asked intensely.

'The truth,' he replied mildly. 'What else?'

'Oh, yes?' She eyed him dangerously. 'She's going to love that! What mum would? Besides which she's sure to think I...conned you into it, somehow.'

He turned into a leafy street in Ascot, a hilly suburb of Brisbane with views of the Brisbane river and some wonderful old houses. 'You never know with my mother. She's not easy to shock.'

'That's why she's a judge, I presume!' Lee rather savagely retorted.

'Could be.' He turned into a driveway and stopped the car.

His fiancée scanned the house before them, and groaned.

He put his arm along the back of her seat and raised an eyebrow at her. 'What now?'

'I might have known! Look, this is just too much! First of all you appropriate my car keys while I'm asleep—which is pretty much like kidnapping me and holding me to ransom so I'm forced to fall in with your wishes—'

'I thought it would save time and argument, that's all,' he said smoothly.

She favoured him with her darkest expression. 'And now,' she continued, 'I'm expected to beard a lady judge who lives in one of Brisbane's National Heritage treasures, by the look of it, and who is quite likely to flip when she discovers I'm her prospective daughter-in-law!'

'It is not a National Heritage treasure, although it is quite old,' he responded.

'Huh!' Lee stared through the windscreen at the elegant two-storeyed redbrick house, with its impressive chimneys and lattice windows, and the spacious grounds that surrounded it.

'As a matter of fact, it was some settler's dream of re-creating a little bit of England in the antipodes. It was quite impractical for the subtropics until we put in air-conditioning,' he added. 'And if you find it impressive, at least you're dressed for the occasion.'

'I am not dressed for the occasion,' she denied, running her hands down her dress. 'I'm dressed for a party! She'll think I'm crazy, arriving for morning tea looking like this.' She tugged at the heart-shaped neck.

'She might have thought *I* was crazy if you'd come in your jeans and boots complete with your string bag,' he pointed out. 'And I did offer you one of my shirts to wear over your dress if it concerned you to that extent.'

'Straight out of *Pretty Woman*,' Lee commented with irony. 'That's why I refused. You probably didn't see the movie, but she was a prostitute.'

'I see.'

Lee was silent for a time, examining the twisted logic of her refusal to wear his shirt over her dress because it made her think of a prostitute. Without it she probably looked like one at this time of day.

She shook her head frustratedly, then said with a frown, 'Does she know about Cyril's will?'

'No. She's been overseas for the last six months on extended leave.'

'Is this the first time you've seen her since she got back?'

'Yes, as a matter of fact it is.'

'That makes me feel really comfortable,' Lee remarked. 'Is there no way I can persuade you to turn this car around and drive off?'

'No. Look, I can't leave her to read about it in the papers. And perhaps I could stiffen *your* resolve somewhat. Just think of Cosmo Delaney.'

'Your fiancée!'

Evelyn Moore tottered to a chair and sat down with her hand to her heart.

Lee drew an embarrassed breath and looked around. The room they were in was straight out of another era. There were heavy garnet velvet curtains at the mullioned windows, a patterned carpet, plenty of mahogany and walnut around, even palms in brass pots that resembled spittoons. There were sepia prints of Brisbane in its infancy; there were parchment vellum shades with garnet velvet trim on the lamps.

She guessed it had been preserved as a living testament to the history of the house, because no one in their right mind would furnish a room this way today—even assuming they could get their hands on the uncomfortable horsehair-stuffed sofas and all the other memorabilia.

Which made her wonder if Damien's mother was a history buff or just a little eccentric—because this room deserved a tasselled rope at the door and a discreet notice not to enter it. It was not a room you entertained guests in.

She switched her gaze back to Evelyn Moore. As tall as her son, she looked to be in her sixties. She had beautifully styled smooth grey hair and his fine dark eyes. She was big-boned, with a regal if not to say autocratic bearing. She wore navy linen trousers and a peacock-blue cotton shirt tucked into them. A sapphire the size of a small pigeon egg adorned her left hand. You could just picture her in a black gown and wig, presiding over the court in a stylish but definitely no-nonsense manner.

This news, however, appeared to have knocked the stuffing out of Justice Moore.

'I don't believe it,' she said faintly. 'Who is she and when did this happen? What about Julia?'

Lee flashed Damien a *told-you-so* look from beneath her lashes.

But his reply to his mother startled her.

'Why are we in here?' he asked coolly. 'Isn't this the room we all laugh about and call the torture chamber?'

His mother looked about her dazedly. 'You know your father insisted we preserve it.'

'Granted, but when do we ever entertain in it?'

'I...' Evelyn gestured and appeared to force herself to look at Lee. 'I think I must have had some premonition this was going to be difficult,' she said slowly.

'Mrs Moore.' Lee spoke for the first time since being introduced. 'It's only to be a marriage of convenience. To be honest, I was in two minds about it myself, but if you'd let Damien explain it might set your mind to rest.'

Evelyn Moore's dark eyes drifted down Lee, taking in the low neckline of her dress, the shortness of her skirt, the bareness of her legs and the height of her heels, the rhinestones. She then appeared to shudder faintly. 'All right, come into the morning room—but this had better be good, Damien!' she warned.

The morning room was chintzy and comfortable and had a bay window looking out over the garden.

Lee sat on a cushion on the window seat and studied the garden as Damien took his mother through the events that had led up to their forthcoming marriage.

'But why on earth would he make such a bequest?' she protested at the end. 'It doesn't make sense.'

'My sentiments entirely,' Lee murmured.

'I notice you didn't knock it back! And why did you agree to marry Damien?' Evelyn replied acidly.

'*I* made the suggestion we do that,' Damien drawled. 'Would it be too much to ask for a cup of coffee?'

'Yes! But you may pour me a gin and tonic, or something. I certainly need a drink!'

'Beloved, your wish is my command,' her son replied, and left the room.

'There has got to be more to it than a deranged bequest in a will!' Evelyn said passionately to Lee. 'You don't look to be his kind of girl at all! Well, not the kind of girl he'd marry.' Once again Evelyn took in Lee's *décolletage*, the coltish grace of her long legs, the luxurious splendour of her hair.

'Thank you,' Lee said politely. 'I won't bore you with the details, but I don't normally go about dressed like this at ten o'clock in the morning. However, you're right. I'm not the kind of girl your son would marry.'

'So?' Evelyn gazed at her imperiously.

'Look,' Lee responded evenly, '*I'm* only doing it so I can rescue my grandparents from penury.' She explained what had happened in more detail.

'You must have been mad to think Cyril Delaney would do that,' Evelyn said incredulously.

'Yes, well, we haven't got to the bottom of that little mystery yet,' Lee replied dryly.

'What exactly are you?' Evelyn enquired with unmistakable hauteur.

Lee looked ruefully down at her dress. 'I'm not some sort of good-time girl. I'm a landscape gardener, in fact. Incidentally, it's not too late to prune your Strelitzia, or bird of paradise, right back. You'd still get a much better showing in a few months. And are you aware that some people are allergic to the spores of the tree fern? I think you have a few much too close to the house. They're so fine, the spores. They blow everywhere and create a lot of dust, don't they?'

Evelyn closed her mouth, which had progressively dropped open during Lee's lecture, just as Damien returned to the room bearing a silver tray.

'I take it you two have locked horns,' he said with a wicked glint in his eye. 'I must warn you, Mother, it is extremely difficult to win an argument with Lee.'

Evelyn shook her head distractedly and took the glass he offered her. She sipped, then said strongly, 'Damien, how can you possibly expect me to give you my blessing on this?'

His dark glance on his mother was suddenly tinged with impatience. But he said evenly, 'It's not exactly a "blessing" event. It's a business transaction. But for what it's worth, I believe you knew Cyril—and he, so he said, admired you.'

Evelyn stared at him open-mouthed. Then she coloured faintly and said disjointedly, 'Yes, I did know him. He...I believe he had a bit of a...' She ran out of words.

'A bit of a crush on you?' her son suggested. And when his mother looked embarrassed, added, 'He obviously had excellent taste.'

Evelyn Moore looked even more embarrassed, then faintly gratified.

'Would you say, ethically, he was above reproach?' Damien asked then.

'Well, yes. I mean he did have a quirky sense of humour at times, but—'

'But you wouldn't have suspected him of making deranged bequests in his will?'

'No.' Evelyn said this definitely, then saw the trap. 'That is to say…' She stopped frustratedly.

'For some reason,' Damien said, 'he wanted us—more probably Lee than myself—to have Plover Park. He felt she needed someone to give her a helping hand. He may even have envisaged the will being contested—incidentally, do you know Cosmo Delaney?'

'Never heard of him,' Evelyn responded promptly. 'But I wouldn't discount Cyril wanting you in the will as much as…Lee,' she added. 'You are my son and…and Cyril never married.' She fiddled with her sapphire, staring down at it intently.

For a moment Lee found herself transported outside the boundaries of this difficult interview as she contemplated Cyril Delaney holding a lifelong torch for Damien's mother. She moved suddenly in a gesture of relief, because if that were so, as Evelyn had implied, it made more sense of Cyril's will…

Damien stared at his mother for a long moment, then was silent, looking into the distance for a time. Finally he shrugged. 'Anyway, that is what I will be doing. After the twelve months is up, Lee will be in the clear and we'll dissolve the marriage.'

'And, to completely set your mind at rest, Mrs Moore,' Lee said, 'your son is quite safe from me.' She cast Damien a dark little glance.

'Well,' Evelyn said, 'I suppose in that case…' She shrugged so eloquently she might as well have shouted…*that doesn't mean to say I have to like the idea at all*…

'The other point to consider,' Damien reflected, 'is this.

Lee has gone from being virtually penniless to a person of quite some substance.'

'What's that supposed to mean?' Lee asked.

He looked her over critically, then smiled suddenly. 'I have no objection to sharing Plover Park with you, Lee. But I have no intention of coping with men on the make who could complicate our partnership considerably.'

Lee gasped. 'You mean—?'

'I mean the best interests of Plover Park could become— muddled—if you suddenly got a man in your life who didn't see eye to eye with me.'

Lee shut her mouth with a click at the same time as Evelyn said judiciously, 'I suppose you have a point.'

Lee found her voice at last. 'You didn't mention that yesterday.'

'I didn't think you'd appreciate it,' he drawled.

'I don't! I'm not some impressionable kid—I can't believe you thought that!'

'It's been known to happen,' Evelyn Moore said dryly.

'Oh! This is too much, really. First he steals my car keys from me, then you treat me like something the cat dragged in—'

Damien forestalled the rest of her tirade by handing her a glass of gin and tonic, then he fished her car keys from his pocket and gave them to her. 'There you go. You're a free agent now.'

'Would someone explain to me what you're talking about?' Evelyn requested in a martyred voice.

Damien turned to his mother. 'We had a slight tussle of wills this morning, that's all. So, do you two think you could see eye to eye over gardens, if nothing else?' He encompassed them both in his suddenly authoritative dark gaze. 'This marriage has no choice but to proceed. I think I told you that my mother is a great admirer of Capability Brown,' he added to Lee, 'and a dedicated gardener despite being at fault over her Strelitzia and tree ferns.'

It amused him to see the two women at present in his life exchange identical looks of feminine outrage. It amused him further to see the exact moment when the irony that they might be united over anything hit them. Then it struck him that these two women were exceptional in their own way.

Instead of being further miffed, they both glanced at him, then glanced at each other. And when his mother asked Lee if she'd like a tour of the garden, Lee responded quietly that she would.

'Well?'

They were driving away from the Ascot house when Damien posed the one-word question.

Lee raised an eyebrow at him.

'What did you think of her?'

'We…got along quite well.' Lee replied primly. Evelyn had adroitly managed to get Lee on her own during their tour of the garden by requesting her son to remove the large wooden cover of the swimming pool filter plant which had got jammed—so jammed it had taken him half an hour of heavy exertion and the implementation of levers to move it, thus allowing Lee and Evelyn time for an in-depth chat.

He said something inaudible, then, 'If you think ganging up on me with my mother is going to get you anywhere, Lee, you're mistaken.'

She smiled fleetingly. 'What gives you that idea?'

'You both looked,' he replied coolly, 'like cats that had got the cream.'

This time Lee grimaced. 'I wouldn't say we've ganged up. At least we know where we stand now, that's all.'

'Where exactly is that?' he queried sardonically.

She glanced at him. 'You probably don't want to know, Damien.'

He engaged the gears and drove the Porsche up a hill with a roar.

He also said dryly, 'The only two people who need to

know where we stand are you and I, Lee.' He accelerated down the other side of the hill.

Lee clutched the armrest. 'I didn't know you had a temper, Damien. Do you really want to get a speeding fine?'

He slowed down, shook his head and looked at her ironically. 'It's just that women are incomprehensible at times—you and my mother included. What nonsense did you concoct between the two of you?'

Lee took exception to his jibe, as well as the bit about nonsense—she was still smarting from discovering the reason for Damien deciding to marry her, anyway—and she said tartly, before she stopped to think, 'Your mother thinks there's a bit more to your decision to marry me. She filled me in on a bit of your life history. She feels your last affair, with Julia—who she approved of much more than she would ever approve of me, incidentally—must have ended disastrously, with you being unable to offer Julia the commitment she was seeking. And that I—along with Cyril's bequest—popped into your life at a strategic moment whereby you could teach this girl a lesson.'

The look Damien Moore cast her was one of sublime amazement, then he started to laugh.

'If anyone should be a good authority on the subject, it's your mother,' Lee said stiffly.

'How wrong you are,' he drawled. 'Is there more?'

'Well...' She hesitated. 'We decided it was fortuitous that it should have been *me* to come into your life at this time.'

'Why is that?'

'Because I am...that is to say, I have no designs on you whatsoever.'

He stopped at a traffic light, eyed her profile, which was in virtuous mode, and grinned suddenly. 'Funny you should say that. I thought last night was touch and go for both of us.'

Colour flooded her cheeks and she stared straight ahead.

'Forget about that?' he queried blandly.

She swallowed. 'In the light of today, it was an aberration.'

'I'm not so sure,' he said reflectively. 'Mind you, you have ten months to prove your stance on this matter.'

She couldn't help herself. She swung her head to look at him, wide-eyed. 'What do you mean?'

'Ten months to prove that you are unmoved by me and have no designs on me.'

'Damien,' she warned, 'don't let this be what I think it is!'

'What's that?' He turned the car into the driveway that led to the underground garage of his apartment block.

'A challenge! A game men play with women! Your mother thought there could be a touch of that in this as well.'

He drove through the automatic gate and brought the Porsche to a smooth stop beside her second-hand yellow Toyota with its several dents. He switched the engine off but made no move to get out.

'My mother may be a judge,' he said pensively, 'but she's the last person to judge my state of mind accurately. As for you, Lee Westwood...' a faint smile touched his mouth '...you don't even know where to begin.'

There wasn't much room in the Porsche. Far too little room to escape the full force of Damien Moore's personality and physical presence. And whilst she might have given rise to the thought in others that she was a tart, kitted out as she was, *he* had gone to visit his mother all present and correctly attired for a Saturday morning. Jeans and a white polo shirt, both fresh from the laundry. A tidy head of hair and freshly shaved. No discernible aftershave but a faint aroma of soap.

Though a stint in the sun wrestling with his mother's pool filter cover had subtly altered the equation...

The same clever dark eyes that could view you with inner amusement, speculation or scepticism, of course. The same lean lines and wide shoulders and those long nice hands. But his labours at the poolside had added a heady smidgen of pure man. His dark hair was awry, there were patches of sweat on his shirt—and it all made him infinitely more dangerous, she realised. It brought home his strength. It made you realise he was physically tough as well as mentally so.

Perhaps it had something to do with the way she was dressed—it certainly didn't help to have so much of her body on display beneath that wandering gaze—but the vibes between them in the closed confines of the car were suddenly threaded with sensual tension.

She moved restlessly. He looked at her from beneath half-closed lids and slid his arm along the back of the seat so he was able to rest his fingertips on the nape of her neck.

Lee swallowed, but she couldn't tear her eyes from his and she couldn't control the tremor that ran through her from her scalp to her toes.

'I gather I annoyed you earlier?' he said softly, dropping his gaze to the heart-shaped edge of her bodice.

She blinked and pressed her hands together as those wandering fingers slipped down the side of her throat towards the valley between her breasts. She tried valiantly to concentrate on what he was saying—but it was a vain effort and she could only stare at him bewilderedly.

'When I intimated that you could fall prey to men on the make if you weren't married to me,' he said. 'It's not as impossible as you seem to think, Lee, with someone who knows what he's doing.'

Belated comprehension came to her. There she was, sitting like a stunned mullet while he explored her body more and more intimately—no, a stunned mullet was not a good analogy, because she was feeling quite the contrary. Alive with delicious anticipation and all sorts of wonderful sensations starting to course through her was a far more accurate description—but...oh, the unfairness of it! she thought bitterly.

Here he was, trying to prove to her that she was a weak, impressionable female any experienced man could touch up, and the one explanation that she could offer in her defence was the last one she could ever use. No other man had a hope in hell of making her feel the way he did!

She breathed raggedly, and did manage to inject a little glint of defiance into her gaze, but all it did was cause him to look amused. Then, just at the moment when she was gathering all her defences because she was sure he was going to kiss her, and she was consumed by dread that she wouldn't be able to resist, he took his hand away and straightened.

'Enough of this,' he murmured, and opened his door.

Surprise made her say incautiously, 'What?'

He looked back at her over his shoulder as he started to get out. 'Smooching in cars is a bit passé—juvenile, whatever—but if you really want to—'

'I would have died rather than kiss you!' she pronounced, controlling her voice rigidly so that all it projected was withering scorn.

He raised his eyebrows, but said gravely, 'Then you won't mind if we proceed upstairs? I'm expecting a phone call.'

There was something extremely undignified in the way she scrambled out of the car—all legs, elbows, flying hair and scarlet-faced as she grappled with the compelling desire to get to Damien Moore and scratch his eyes out.

Fortunately, before she succeeded in this ambition, sanity returned. It was still an uncomfortable ride up in the lift to his apartment, though. She was still breathing a little raggedly and looking like a red-haired thunder cloud, whereas he seemed to be entirely relaxed as he leant against the lift wall and studied her casually.

'I'll just get my things and go,' she said frostily as he unlocked the door.

'No need to rush off. Wouldn't you care to change first?'

Lee clicked her tongue and looked down at herself, annoyed.

'All right.'

'I'll make us the coffee we missed out on in the meantime.'

'I'm not staying around to drink coffee with you for

hours,' she warned. 'I've got a nursery to run and I wasn't expecting to be away this long anyway.'

'I'll try to keep it as brief as possible,' he replied gravely.

Lee opened her mouth, then turned on her heel and marched away in the direction of the spare bedroom.

Once she was changed, she sat down on the end of the bed and looked around. If, she thought acidly, his last affair had ended disastrously, as his mother had briefed her, whose clothes and cosmetics were taking up space in this room? A part-time lover? A career woman who was not looking for commitment, perhaps, as opposed to a serious mistress or a serious relationship?

She bit her lip on discovering she didn't like the thought of that one bit. Why? Because it made him the kind of man she didn't approve of, or…? Stop there, Lee Westwood, she ordered herself. This is going to be hard enough without getting jealous over some faceless woman!

She picked up her string bag, and the carrier bag she'd packed her new clothes into, and sallied forth, determined to blot Damien Moore's spare bedroom and its contents from her mind.

She found him in his study, a book-lined room complete with desk and all sorts of computerware. He was behind the desk, but there was a big leather armchair and on the low table in front of it there was tray set with one cup and plunger pot of coffee.

He was working at the computer as she came in, and had already poured his coffee, but he sat back and looked her over thoroughly. 'That's better,' he remarked, his lips twisting.

Lee looked down at herself in her T-shirt, jeans and boots. Her hair was tied back in a ponytail and her green scarf was draped around her neck. She frowned. 'What do you mean? You gave me to understand you didn't approve of my clothes, and now you seem to be saying you didn't approve of these!' She raised the carrier bag to bring it to his attention, then dropped it to the floor with a plop to signify righteous indignation.

'It's not that I didn't approve of them,' he said meditatively. 'I just…have some affection for your one-woman SWAT team model, I guess.'

Lee stared at him with her nose somewhat pinched. 'You're a hard man to please,' she said, and sat down.

'I didn't mean to offend you.'

'Not in the least,' she denied untruthfully. 'So. What was it you said you'd be as brief as possible about? And I mean really brief.' She glanced at her watch.

'All right. Are we still going to get married, and, if so, where and when?'

'I…' She fiddled unconsciously with the diamond on her left hand, 'I don't know.'

'Still having second thoughts, Lee?'

'I'm just thinking—it sounds fine on paper,' she said intensely, 'but take your moving into Plover Park, for example. You could be bored stiff. It's very quiet. It's country! There are mice, possums, spiders—even snakes.'

'I can't claim to like them, but a snake or two has never bothered me.'

Lee poured her coffee and sighed. 'I wish I could think of some other way to do this.'

'There is—you could move in with me.'

She stared at him out of stunned eyes, shocked into speechlessness.

'Then there isn't another way, Lee,' he said. Something in the way he said it made her feel suddenly wary. As if she was looking down the barrel of a gun, for example. And she remembered his words of the previous day about what his simplest course of action would be.

'Then I'll leave it up to you to arrange the wedding—just no church,' she said quietly.

'All right. It'll probably take about two weeks to organise, and I'd really appreciate it if you could come up here for it. I'm going to be absolutely flat to the boards getting all my ends tied up so I can get away.'

She grimaced inwardly and it occurred to her to wonder how she would break this news to her grandparents. Perhaps it would be best to just do it and leave the explanations until after the fact. She said slowly, 'Yes, I will.' She looked around. 'Don't blame me if you find yourself hating Plover Park, though.' She stood up and picked up her things.

He surprised her. He said, 'I'm actually looking forward to it. I need a break.' He gestured at the computer, then folded his hands behind his head.

'Do you have any special dietary requirements?' she asked.

'Nope—uh—well—' he eyed her comically '—I don't eat like a rabbit.'

'So I noticed, so long as someone else cooks for you,' she returned with some asperity.

'Oh, I can cook,' he drawled. 'I just don't have the time, normally. But I won't be a burden to you in that department if that's what's worrying you. Cutting into your valuable time by demanding you prepare meals for me like a good little wife, for example,' he said wickedly.

'Then I'll see you when I see you,' she replied, with as much disdain as she was capable of, and started to stalk out of the room.

'I hesitate to destroy your exit, Lee—' he got up leisurely '—but you can't get out of the garage without my key. I'll come down with you.'

She closed her eyes frustratedly.

He grinned and came over to take her hand. 'I guess you're having one of those days.'

'I guess I am,' she answered sadly.

'Never mind. Things can only improve.'

She looked up at him and straightened her shoulders, but they slumped almost immediately.

'Hey,' he said softly, 'you're going home to your beloved nursery.'

'Of course!' But it came out gruffly, and to her horror she had to blink away a tear or two. 'Sorry.' She pulled out a hanky and blew her nose. 'I think I've had too many shocks in too short a period. I never cry normally.' She tucked the hanky back into her jeans pocket. 'OK. Lead on MacDuff!'

But he didn't immediately lead her down to the garage. He put his arms around her waist and rested his chin on the top of her head for a moment. 'Don't worry,' he said quietly, 'I won't let Cosmo hurt you.' Then he kissed her on the lips.

Lee stood stock still in the circle of his arms and accepted his kiss. She didn't exactly respond, but that was only because it ended before she could do anything other than find herself flooded—mentally and physically—with an incredible sense of longing to stay put in Damien Moore's arms. To stay put in his apartment and experience to the full the kind of magic being his lover would bring...

But he released her and said whimsically, 'Let's go, José. You've got a long drive ahead of you.'

It turned out to be an even longer drive, as Lee took a wrong turning and had some difficulty in finding an on-ramp to the Pacific Motorway.

Concentrate! she commanded herself. You're carrying on like a starstruck kid and it won't do! It's not as if *he's* feeling like jelly inside and all shook up...

Several days later she received a note from Damien, confirming the wedding date. Attached to the note was a cutting from the *Sunday Mail* society column: a picture of her in Damien's arms at Ella Patroni's *Gilligan's Island* party. It was a flattering picture. Her black dress looked both sexy and chic, *she* looked long-legged, sexy and chic—the only problem was she also looked besotted as she gazed up at her tall partner. In fact, the caption said it all… *The Secret Fiancée—but obviously in love!*

She ground her teeth. In his note, Damien made no mention of the cutting or the caption. Did he, she wondered, put it down to great acting? A hollow little feeling inside her told her that Damien Moore was far too clever and experienced with women to buy that completely. But what to do about it?

She discovered she had no idea.

Two weeks after the party, she returned to his apartment for her wedding.

She had no idea what to expect, although she had taken some care with her appearance. Another new dress—simple but stylish, and green to match her eyes—worn with ivory shoes. Her hair was up, his aunt's diamond was on her finger. But there was a surprise waiting for her. A small bouquet of exquisite Cooktown orchids—provided by her husband-to-be, who looked breathtakingly handsome in a fawn suit and a dark brown shirt—and Ella and Hank Patroni.

They accompanied them to the register office and acted as witnesses, then took them back to the penthouse where a sumptuous lunch had been set up. And somehow Ella contrived to ignore all the peculiarities of this wedding—including Damien's mother's absence—and turn it into a festive occasion.

Ella did say that big weddings were absolutely exhausting for those who had to organise them and she was sure this was a better way to go, and she did take Lee aside and assure her that Evelyn Moore would come round eventually, not to worry, giving Lee to understand that this was how Damien had explained this low-key affair to her.

But Lee had been struck by a tinge of guilt, and for a mad moment was tempted to explain the true nature of her marriage to Damien Moore. She didn't, however. Then, after the lunch, she and Damien were alone in his apartment.

'That wasn't so bad, was it?'

Lee turned to him. She'd been studying the view of the river. 'No,' she said quietly. 'And thank you for the flowers and for allowing Ella to organise a lunch. But I felt a bit sneaky.'

He grimaced, formed a fist and touched it lightly to the point of her jaw. 'This may be a business transaction, Lee, but we don't need to adopt a hole-and-corner approach. I don't think I told you how attractive you look, by the way, Mrs Moore.'

Lee trembled to think of herself as Mrs Damien Moore. And she remembered how, at the critical moment in the register office, just before he'd slid a gold wedding band on to her finger, Damien had kissed her lightly and said beneath his breath, 'Don't worry, it's going to be OK.'

And perhaps, from the understanding of things she had given him, he really believed that. How different a matter would it be if he could see into her heart?

She said, 'Thanks,' and tried to look humorous. 'Two new dresses in two weeks!'

He grinned. 'At least I'm having a beneficial effect on the state of your wardrobe! What would you like to do now?'

She breathed a little uncertainly. 'I think…I'll go home.'

'You don't have to, Lee.' He frowned.

'Damien—' she swallowed '—Plover Park is the place I feel happiest—happier than I've been for a long time.' She twirled her rings. 'That's why I did this. So, if you wouldn't mind, I will go home. When will you come down?'

He hesitated briefly. 'I'm going to need another week to organise myself up here.'

'Well, I'll see you then. Thanks again for doing all this so nicely.'

'Lee…' He paused and looked in two minds for a moment, then, 'It was a pleasure. Drive carefully, Mrs Moore.'

A week later, Plover Park looked its best.

With her grandparents' help the house had been spring-cleaned, the gardens glowed and the nursery was spick and span.

There was no doubt it was a desirable property. Its tree-studded paddocks rolled gently down to a creek. Some stately Murray Grey cows and five playful calves roamed the paddocks, and shared the creek with a variety of birdlife—including, at this time, a family of ducks. The creek meandered in secretive loops and bends between giant camphor laurels and was often studded with water lilies.

The house, which she and Damien had inherited jointly, had come to them furnished, and Cyril Delaney's taste had been impeccable. It would be fair to say that Lee loved both the house and its furniture.

The house was of sandstone bricks, its main rooms surrounding a brick fireplace that soared beneath wooden cathedral ceilings to a chimney set in a little tower above the sage green roof. The vast lounge and dining room on one side of the fireplace looked across an open flagged terrace towards the creek. The kitchen, on the other side, overlooked a covered veranda, a colourful garden, guarded by a huge box pine, and the orchard. The bedrooms were in two wings at an angle to the central area.

The inside walls were unpainted brick and the furniture was solid but elegant, yet minimalist. All the rooms had lovely views—even the main bedroom's *en-suite* bathroom, where you could lie in the bath and watch the birds and the cows. There was not only plenty of wild birdlife at Plover Park, but Lee had also acquired four chickens and a rooster, and three guinea fowl which she treated as pets.

On the day she expected Damien Moore to move in, she had a long chat with her guinea fowl…

'Now listen here, Roly, Hermione and Lydia,' she said as she scattered breadcrumbs for them, 'I think I've told you that if I'd known how noisy guinea fowl can be I may have thought twice about buying you. Mind you, I don't mind your company and your shouting—well, most of the time—but we're having a visitor and he may not be as agreeable to being woken up at the crack of dawn as I am. That goes for you too, Henry,' she added sternly to the rooster. 'And it goes for the whole lot of you in the matter of leaving your calling cards on the verandas!'

'Lee,' her grandmother chided, 'if you didn't feed them around the house you mightn't have the problem!'

They were having their morning tea break. Lee went back to the veranda table, pausing to admire a scarlet poinsettia in full bloom, and sat down with a grin. 'I know. I'm mad! But I like them.' She patted the head of her devoted golden retriever, Peach, who had lived with her grandparents while she'd been in Brisbane, and he laid his muzzle in her lap.

Mary Mercer looked at her granddaughter affectionately, but then her expression clouded. 'Darling, you know your grandfather and I couldn't be more grateful for what you've done, but I'm worried about this turn of events.'

Lee tried to look unconcerned. 'Damien's OK, Nan.'

'Perhaps. But…I'm just not really comfortable with you having to marry him to rescue us—'

'I know,' Lee interrupted ruefully. 'But you had no say in the matter,' she pointed out. 'I did it first and told you later.'

'So you did.' Mary looked pensive. 'If ever there was a chip off the old block, you're it. Your mother also used to rush in where angels feared to tread. Come to that—' she shrugged '—your grandfather is the same.'

'Thanks,' Lee said wryly. 'But, Nan, it's done—so please don't worry about it.'

'I'm not so much worried about the fact of it at the moment, but I sense some inner turmoil for you,' Mary said slowly. 'Did you do just what Cyril Delaney may have intended to happen, darling?' she asked gently.

Lee's eyes flew to her grandmother's. She might have inherited her mother and grandfather's impetuosity, but she'd inherited her grandmother's eye colour. And she could see in those now faded green eyes that her grandmother's intuition where she was concerned was alive and working well...

She looked away with a sigh. 'I don't know what I really think of Damien Moore,' she said gruffly. 'I did...I did once think I was in love with him. I have no idea how Cyril may have divined that, or even if he did, but, yes, I'm in some difficulty over Damien.'

'Could it be that he's in some difficulty over you?'

Lee blinked. 'He's *never* given me the slightest indication that he could be in love with me.'

'He married you,' Mary said quietly.

Lee shrugged. 'Until this raised its ugly head he had no intention of marrying me.'

'Men can be cynical—especially men who may have had a lot of women running after them,' Mary offered.

'Men—especially men like Damien—are a serious threat to womanhood,' Lee replied with a spark of humour. 'Nan, it's probably just that. You get those irresistible men, like a virus, then one day you wake up to find it's all out of your system!'

'I hope so, dear—oh, there you are, Bill!' she said as Lee's grandfather strode round the corner of the house. 'Come and have your tea!'

Bill Mercer ruffled Lee's hair in passing and sat down. At the same time a metallic blue Porsche drove past the box pine and pulled up.

'Damn fine car!' her grandfather pronounced. 'I wonder if he'll let me look under the bonnet?'

Lee and Mary exchanged wry glances, because cars tended to supersede all else for Bill Mercer.

'I'm seriously impressed.'

They were sitting on the terrace, just Lee and Damien. Mary and Bill had gone home to their house in the nearby village.

'Thanks.' Lee replied. There was a CD of romantic classics

playing softly in the background and her guinea fowl and chickens were fossicking around on the smooth green lawn beyond the terrace. The sky was a deep blue above them, the shadows of the trees were lengthening across the paddocks, and the warm clear air had that special radiance lent to it by a setting sun.

Lee had a glass of wine; Damien was drinking a beer. Dinner—a pasta marinara for which Damien had brought all the ingredients with him and had concocted himself—was under control. The table on the terrace was set.

Damien looked across at her. She'd had a shower and changed into clean jeans and a white blouse. There was no doubt in his mind that she was trying to project a relaxed air, but he could see the tension beneath it.

He said, 'Why don't you have your grandparents living here with you?'

'My grandmother really loves her home and garden and she's prone to migraines if she gets too unsettled. They're happy to look after the place for me if I need to be away, but I don't want to uproot her if I can avoid it.'

'But don't you get lonely or feel unsafe?'

Lee looked around and whistled softly. Peach immediately came running round the corner of the house to sit adoringly at her feet.

Damien grinned. 'OK, but what about lonely?'

'I don't think I've had time to feel lonely. And besides Peach I've got my birds.'

'Tell me about them,' he invited, studying the mixture of guinea fowl and chickens on the lawn.

'The hens go by the names of Shirley, Hattie, Flojo and Merlene. The rooster is Henry, because he reminds me of Henry VIII—he'll add any passing chook to his harem! The two dark grey guinea fowl are Hermione and Roly; the pale grey one is Lydia. Lydia hates Henry, and often chases him and pulls feathers out of his tail.'

He looked amused. 'Why?'

'Well...' Lee gestured. 'It's rather sad. Unlike Henry, Roly is a one-girl man. He and Hermione are inseparable. They tolerate Lydia, but never let her get too close. So she's a frustrated spinster and she often goes about haranguing the whole world. Arrogant males, which Henry definitely is, are anathema to her. Incidentally, guineas in haranguing mode are unmelodic and deafening, I should warn you!'

'Thanks. Go on, this is fascinating.'

Lee glanced at him, but there was nothing about his expression to suggest he wasn't being genuine. She chuckled softly. 'That was my scenario, I should say, until I found out that Lydia, who was sold to me as a girl, is in fact a bloke.'

Damien sat up and studied the pale grey guinea fowl. 'How can you tell?'

'Male guineas have larger horns and wattles. But the one true test of femininity in Numida Meleagris, or the African Guinea Fowl, is in their call. Only the female utters the two-syllable call that sounds like ''Go-back, Go-back!'' And only Hermione makes that call here.'

He burst out laughing. 'So Lydia is a Lionel?'

'Except that I can't stop thinking of him as a she and I can't change his name. And he's still the odd man out, although it does explain why he feels he can take Henry on.' Lee stood up. 'Should I check the pasta? I—'

'Sit down,' he recommended. 'I'll do it.'

'But—'

'But me no buts!' He got up and strolled inside.

Lee sank back into her chair and examined the unreality of it all.

Here they were, just the two of them, a married couple in everything *but* reality. OK, it had been an easy enough day, she reflected. He'd been perfectly happy with the bedroom that she'd prepared for him at the opposite end of the house to hers. He'd expressed his appreciation of the desk she'd set up for him in the family room, which had a telephone line so he could access his e-mail and use his laptop computer. He'd spent most of the afternoon helping her grandfather to repair the pump that drew water from the creek to the nursery.

Then Bill and Mary had departed and he'd taken over the kitchen to prepare dinner, showing a culinary expertise that had caused her eyes to widen. But what was ahead? she wondered, uneasily. She rose with the sun, which was roughly five-thirty at this time of the year, and after a long full day went to bed at nine o'clock. For some reason she couldn't picture Damien Moore being an early to rise, early to bed type, so…

'Lee?'

She jumped, and turned to see him standing in the terrace doorway, studying her humorously.

'What?'

'Don't look so worried! All you have to do is your own thing and I'll do mine.'

'I…I…' She couldn't go on, and could have killed herself as she twisted her hands awkwardly.

A wry smile touched his mouth. 'Just think of us as housemates,' he recommended. 'And I'm ready to serve dinner if you're ready to eat.'

'I…thank you, yes,' she said helplessly.

CHAPTER FIVE

'I'M GOING to spray the cows this morning,' Lee said to Damien at breakfast. 'It should be done every six weeks at this time of the year, for buffalo fly.'

'I'll give you a hand.' He passed her the toast.

Not only had he cooked the most divine pasta marinara the night before, he'd cooked breakfast this morning. Bacon, eggs and fried tomatoes. Her sole contribution had been a fragrant pot of percolated coffee. In fact it had been the aroma of bacon that she'd woken up to—she'd slept in and Damien had been up before her.

'Did you sleep all right?' she'd asked anxiously on encountering him shaved, showered and dressed in khaki shorts and shirt, although barefoot.

'Like a baby,' he'd replied. And he'd certainly looked relaxed, as well as very much at home. He'd let the chickens and guinea fowl out, collected the eggs and fed Peach.

It was rather difficult for Lee to associate him in this role with his other persona the hotshot lawyer. It even led her to reflect that this might not be such a disaster after all from the point of view of how he would fit in with her lifestyle at Plover Park.

The previous evening had been...comfortable, she thought. After dinner they'd gone for a walk in the extended twilight of daylight saving, then they'd watched television until she'd yawned and been told by him to go to bed and not to worry about him. She'd hesitated, then done as she was told. What he'd occupied himself with she had no idea; she'd fallen asleep as soon as her head had touched the pillow.

Now she said, 'I can manage the cows. That's one thing about Murray Greys; they're very amenable.'

'Surely two pairs of hands are better than one?'

They were eating on the veranda outside the kitchen. Peach was sitting beside Lee, thumping his tail now and then in case he should be forgotten in the matter of scraps. Lee handed him a bacon rind and picked up her coffee cup.

The garden was still sparkling beneath a diamond coating of dew as the rising sun cast its rays around. The sky was clear, birds were singing, and it was going to be a brilliant day. She cast her eyes contentedly along the rockery that bordered the drive. Six rose bushes, from deep velvety red through to a lovely clear yellow, were blooming extravagantly.

'OK,' she said slowly. 'Just be careful. I've got my neighbour's bull here at the moment. He's really a pussycat most of the time, but he is huge! A lot of accidents with bulls happen when people get crushed against fences and walls.'

'Is that a fact? All right, I'll take care. How long is he here for?'

'Two months. His name—my name for him anyway—is Ferdinand.' She looked mischievous. 'He's a very romantic bull.'

Damien blinked. 'It would appear that nothing that moves escapes being named round here—how so romantic, though?'

'Well, he chooses a cow and he never leaves her side. He even lies down next to her and—I don't know—somehow projects the image of being in love with her.'

'Really?' The fine lines beside Damien's eyes crinkled. 'I gather it doesn't last for ever, though?'

Lee dropped Peach another bacon rind from Damien's plate. 'Only a few days—but at least he knows how to make a girl feel special at the time.'

'I'll bear that in mind.'

Lee looked at him wryly. 'I doubt Ferdy could teach you much, Damien. So,' she continued, without giving him the opportunity to reply, 'here's how we do it. The yard, as you may have noticed, is next to the main gate, and the cows a the moment are in the furthest paddock from the road. I'll mix the stuff up, then I'll take the tractor and some lucerne to the middle gate—once they see me on the tractor, using the lucerne as the proverbial carrot, they generally come running and follow me into the yard.'

'What would you like me to do?'

'Open the middle gate. Why don't you borrow Bill's wellingtons?' For as long as she could remember she'd called her grandfather by his first name, and she pointed to his pair of boots neatly lined up on the veranda. 'Just in case you spook them and they take off across the creek.'

He grimaced. 'Good thinking, Mrs Moore. When do we start?'

'As soon as we've done the dishes—that is, I will do the dishes since you cooked brekky. Thanks.' Lee patted her stomach. 'I haven't had that kind of breakfast for years.'

'Let me guess,' he murmured. 'You're a fruit and muesli girl? Yoghurt?'

'Well—' Lee shrugged '—it is healthy.'

He smiled into her eyes but it was a secretive smile. 'It's also nice to break out and live a bit once in a while.'

'Why do I get the feeling you mean that in a—larger context?' she asked cautiously.

He allowed his dark gaze to drift over her. She wore denim shorts and a faded pink T-shirt with Snoopy on the front and her feet were bare. Her hair was tied back severely and she wore no make-up. There was little evidence that this was the girl he'd taken to Ella Patroni's party. His gaze narrowed on the thought that Lee Westwood was an enigma. Her wholehearted dedication to this project was somewhat at odds with the lifestyles of most of the twenty-four-year-old girls of his acquaintance.

Yet Cyril Delaney had read her right in that he couldn't have put Plover Park into better hands, not to say brought her more pleasure—you couldn't think anything else, he mused. Did that mean Cyril had done his own investigation of Lee Westwood?

And *had* he, Damien Moore, said what he'd just said to her in a larger context? For example trying to merge this dedicated horticulturist turned farmer with the girl who had been such a stunning partner at Ella's party? If so, why? he asked himself. Because he knew he could unsettle her? Knew there were times when she was not as unaffected by him as she'd like him to think? His lips twitched at the thought. Even now he could see her growing restive and bothered beneath his regard…

All the same, what complications would he be adding to those he'd already invited? It had been an uncharacteristically quixotic gesture to suggest this marriage, but as a marriage of convenience it had presented him with little difficulty. Once it became anything more than a marriage in name only, how difficult was it going to be to walk away in ten months' time? Which he had fully, and always intended to do… But was it too late to stem the sensual appreciation of Lee Westwood that had started to trickle into his blood?

He stood up and looked enigmatically at her upturned face with its expression of growing bewilderment that signified she had no idea what was going through his mind. And he had to smile slightly. Because although his wife could be a tiger in lots of respects, she was astonishingly naive in others…

'A larger context?' He shrugged. 'I guess it doesn't hurt anyone to live a little, that's all. What say I meet you at the middle gate in half an hour?'

Lee hesitated as she sensed she was being fobbed off, but something warned her not to probe any further. She gathered the plates and stood up. 'Yes, I should be ready by then. By the way, if you didn't bring a hat—'

'I did.'

'Then you should wear it. It may be early but it's going to be a scorcher.'

'Yes, ma'am,' he said meekly.

She ignored this. 'And take a stick. Not only for the cows but just in case you run across a snake. There's a selection of them in the garage.'

'Certainly, ma'am.' He tugged his forelock.

'That is the worst imitation of a serf I've ever seen!' And she walked indoors, laughing at him out of those stunning green eyes.

It was nearly three quarters of an hour later by the time she jumped onto the tractor. Damien had disappeared, but she'd been delayed by a phone call.

She fired the ancient red Massey Ferguson, checked that her load of a biscuit of lucerne, spray and apparatus was secure on the carry-all, and trundled down the hill from the shed to the main drive, with Peach lolloping along behind her.

She drove over the first cattle grid, and was about to turn left off the drive into the paddock and head towards the middle gate when she looked ahead. There, on the right of the drive, next to the main gate, was the wooden sliprail yard where she'd planned to pen the cattle and spray them—full of cows.

She blinked and nearly stalled the tractor, for there also, lounging against the rails, was Damien Moore. She gritted her teeth. He had single-handedly, and without any inducement, successfully yarded five cows, five very active calves and one very large bull.

'Peach,' she said bitterly, as she recovered herself and drove towards the yard, 'is there anything this man can't turn his hand to?'

To Damien Moore she said, as she pulled up next to the yard and killed the motor, 'I gather there's something you haven't told me? To do with *not* being the city slicker you appear to be?' Her gaze was severe.

He looked amused from beneath his broad-brimmed

Akubra. 'I did a stint of jackerooing in my dim and distant youth, that's all.'

'All! You could have told me.' She vaulted off the tractor. 'I feel a right fool now!'

'Sorry.' His teeth glinted. 'I couldn't resist it. Why don't you tell me their names? I'm sure they have names.'

Lee pulled on some rubber gloves, poured the mixture from the bucket into the spray gun and screwed the top on carefully. 'And that makes me feel about ten years old.'

He straightened as she approached the yard and started to climb over the rails. 'Lee…um…you don't plan to get in there with them, do you?'

'Of course I do!' She balanced on the top rail and reached for the mask that was hanging around her neck.

'I don't know about a ten-year-old, but you're mad,' he said firmly, and wrested the spray from her. 'You were the one that warned me about the dangers of getting crushed!' He gestured impatiently towards the milling, mooing cows trampling around in the small yard.

'But I can't get to the calves properly unless I get in,' Lee objected. 'I'm fast and agile,' she added proudly.

'You may be, but you're still only a slip of a girl.' And he climbed over the rail into the yard.

'I… Oh, well, take my mask.' She held it out to him. 'Watch out for Ferdy!'

But if she was fast and agile Damien did it all by authority, she saw over the next few minutes. Her cows—damn them, she thought acidly—recognised someone who knew what he was doing and reacted accordingly. Then it struck her that they were *their* cows, but it didn't help much.

'OK, mission accomplished,' he said, and opened the yard to release the small herd.

Lee watched them drift out, then cross the drive and, with a sudden excess of spirit, gallop skittishly across the paddock with Ferdy lumbering along behind. She realised Damien was standing next to her.

'Penny for them?' he said.

She sighed. 'I guess I thought there might be one thing I was better at than you are. So I'm feeling a little deflated, but I'll get over it.'

He laughed softly. 'If I've surprised you, you've also surprised me. What did you think of the photo in the paper?'

Her eyes widened and a tinge of colour warmed her cheeks. 'It was...for the purpose of what the rest of the world thinks of us, it was perfect.'

'It was that all right.' He grinned wickedly. 'But what do you think their reaction would be if they could see you now?'

She looked down at herself ruefully. She'd changed out of her shorts and she now had a khaki bush shirt on—purchased from a disposal store and several sizes too big—with faded, patched moleskins and short brown boots. Her hair was tucked up into a floppy khaki hat. 'They could be forgiven for thinking it was a different girl.'

'Precisely. They could even be forgiven for thinking you were a boy, at the moment. But not necessarily a less interesting person.'

She looked into his eyes uncertainly.

'What I'm trying to say is—you are a constant surprise to me.' He sobered. 'But promise me one thing. Don't ever do this on your own again.'

His eyes, she realised, were almost black, and completely compelling. 'I—'

'Not because you're incompetent,' he overrode her, 'but because accidents *can* happen, and with no one around it could be a disaster.'

'I don't usually do it without Bill around,' she confessed.

'Good. What's next on the agenda?'

'I need to spend some time in the nursery. It was a phone call that delayed me, by the way. Bill rang to say that Nan has woken up with a migraine so he's going to keep her quiet and at home for the day. And then I was planning to tackle my bookwork. Why?'

'Could you fit in a swim and lunch at Byron Bay? I'm taking over the new office today, but that's only a matter of getting the keys and having a look around, as well as a short meeting with the interior decorator.'

The one thing Plover Park lacked was a swimming pool. The creek was no more than knee deep, and she already had sweat running down her face beneath her floppy hat as the sun beat down with quite some intensity, despite it only being eight-thirty in the morning. The thought of a swim in the surf at Byron Bay was almost irresistible.

'Well…' she temporised.

'I could lend a hand in the nursery,' he said. 'And I wouldn't mind going over your bookwork with you. I don't see why we couldn't fit it all in.' He traced the droplets of moisture and tendrils of hair stuck to her cheek.

Lee moved for two reasons: the feel of his fingers on her skin and the hollow feeling within that told her Damien intended to get his way over this. He'd pushed his hat back, and because she was still sitting on the rail, with her heels hooked on the rung below, she had the unusual advantage of being able to look down at him. For a moment she was unbearably tempted to return the compliment—to trace the outline of his face, the line of his strong throat and run her fingers across the width of his shoulders beneath the khaki cotton.

It was as if a force she had no control over was gathering within her, propelling her to take her hands off the rail and put them on his shoulders or, even worse, to kiss him. Her breath caught in her throat at the thought and a tide of hunger ran through her. She might look like a boy at the moment, but she'd never felt more like a woman in her life, or been more aware of a man. All her senses were under siege and she felt fragile and vulnerable because of it.

Helpless, she thought chaotically, under the impact of Damien Moore in all his glory—and there was so much glory in him for her. Not only that strong, elegant body, but the way his hair sometimes fell in his eyes, the way those eyes laughed at her, his hands, and the mental vision she often simply couldn't conquer of those hands on her slender body...

'Lee?'

Her green eyes focused to see him looking up at her narrowly, and she took a deep breath. 'Uh...' It took quite a mental wrench to remember what they'd been saying, as well as her distinct reservations about spending time lunching and swimming with him. But, really, what difference was there between doing that with him at Byron Bay and having breakfast with him at Plover Park?

'All right,' she said, and added, striving for a casual approach, 'Sounds cool.'

He smiled absently and his dark eyes lingered on her face for a moment more. Then he straightened and looked at the tractor. 'I haven't driven one of those for years.'

Lee's lips twitched. 'Be my guest. I'll hop on the carry-all.'

'I don't want to usurp all your—'

'Don't worry about it,' she advised. 'I get the feeling you and Bill are kindred spirits in all things mechanical, and to be honest, the pedals are so stiff on this ol' thing—' she patted the red bonnet of the tractor '—my legs sometimes feel as if they're going to seize up!'

He climbed aboard with a grin and she hopped onto the carry-all. Several hours later she was seated beside him in the Porsche, a vastly superior conveyance...

As she'd got ready for the outing she'd experienced more mental turmoil. Her wardrobe left a lot to be desired; her desire to look chic and glamorous and definitely not like a boy left a lot to be explained...

In the matter of clothes she'd finally found a short camellia-pink shift she'd forgotten she owned so long was it since she'd last worn it. But combined with a pair of white sandals and gold hoop earrings in her ears it would do for Byron Bay, which ran the gamut of smart-casual to hippie grunge. She'd put it on over her pale green bikini and packed a towel, sunscreen and a peaked cap into a raffia holdall. She'd left her hair loose and put a pair of sunglasses on the top of her head.

A parade in front of her bedroom mirror had been reassuring. One thing that never let her down was her hair. She'd thought of washing it, but as she'd be swimming it seemed a waste of time. And the dress looked OK. Simple but cool, a lovely colour, and it showed off her legs. Then she had stopped parading in front of the mirror and sat down on the end of the bed to chew her lip anxiously.

Here was she, Lee Westwood, going through all the conventional motions of a girl wanting to impress a man. The should-I-wash-my-hair? motions; the is-this-the-right-dress? indecision; the do-I-need-to-shave-my-legs? tizzy. And all for a man she definitely should not want to be impressing.

The thing is, I can't seem to help myself, she had thought sadly. But I am not being helped by this proximity, and I'm not being helped by Damien himself. There's no need to touch me, no need for him to tantalise me, no need for *double entendres*—no need, come to think of it, for him to be so damn perfect! But...did I bring it on myself to a certain extent? With my little black dress, for example, and the dancing display I gave?

A toot from the Porsche had brought her out of her reverie. She'd picked up her holdall and sallied forth.

Now, as the Porsche ate up the scenic hilly miles between Plover Park and Byron Bay, often lined with macadamia plantations, Damien explained the rationale behind his decision to open a branch there.

'We get a lot of Northern New South Wales business in Brisbane—the nearest big city, but across the border in the state of Queensland. There are differences in state legislation, though—particularly in conveyancing, for example. So an of-

GET FREE BOOKS and a FREE GIFT WHEN YOU PLAY THE...

Just scratch off the silver box with a coin. Then check below to see the gifts you get!

Lucky 7

SLOT MACHINE GAME!

YES! I have scratched off the silver box. Please send me the 2 free Harlequin Presents® books and gift for which I qualify. I understand I am under no obligation to purchase any books, as explained on the back of this card.

306 HDL DRM9

106 HDL DRNQ
(H-P-10/02)

FIRST NAME	LAST NAME

ADDRESS

APT.#	CITY

STATE/PROV.	ZIP/POSTAL CODE

7 7 7	**Worth TWO FREE BOOKS plus a BONUS Mystery Gift!**
🍒 🍒 🍒	**Worth TWO FREE BOOKS!**
♣ ♣ ♣	**Worth ONE FREE BOOK!**
🔔 🔔 🍒	**TRY AGAIN!**

Visit us online at www.eHarlequin.com

The Harlequin Reader Service® — Here's how it works:

Accepting your 2 free books and gift places you under no obligation to buy anything. You may keep the books and gift and return the shipping statement marked "cancel." If you do not cancel, about a month later we'll send you 6 additional novels and bill you just $3.57 each in the U.S., or $4.24 each in Canada, plus 25¢ shipping & handling per book and applicable taxes if any.* That's the complete price and — compared to cover prices of $4.25 each in the U.S. and $4.99 each in Canada — it's quite a bargain! You may cancel at any time, but if you choose to continue, every month we'll send you 6 more books, which you may either purchase at the discount price or return to us and cancel your subscription.

*Terms and prices subject to change without notice. Sales tax applicable in N.Y. Canadian residents will be charged applicable provincial taxes and GST.

If offer card is missing write to: Harlequin Reader Service, 3010 Walden Ave., P.O. Box 1867, Buffalo NY 14240-1867

BUSINESS REPLY MAIL
FIRST-CLASS MAIL   PERMIT NO. 717-003   BUFFALO, NY

POSTAGE WILL BE PAID BY ADDRESSEE

HARLEQUIN READER SERVICE
3010 WALDEN AVE
PO BOX 1867
BUFFALO NY 14240-9952

NO POSTAGE
NECESSARY
IF MAILED
IN THE
UNITED STATES

fice here, with solicitors here conversant with New South Wales legislation, makes sense.'

'I see. I did wonder about that,' she replied.

He looked at her wryly. 'Now you know. Did you think it was devious machination on my part to worm my way into Plover Park?'

She grimaced. 'Not really. Well, serious consideration told me you're too good a businessman and lawyer for that kind of thing.'

He raised his eyebrows. 'That kind of thing?'

She glanced at him, and to her amazement, heard herself say, 'Apart from that, I guess you wouldn't have to go to those lengths for a woman anyway.'

'That is setting the cat amongst the pigeons, Lee,' he remarked after a moment as he turned off the Pacific Highway to take Ross Lane down to the coast.

Don't I know it? she thought, and wished she'd bitten her tongue. She gestured a little awkwardly. 'What I mean is, I'm absolving you of any…suspicious ploys,' she brought out, 'in relation to myself.'

He laughed softly. 'Despite the fact our morals—for want of a better term—get a bit carried away at times?'

She bit her lip and felt herself colour. 'Perhaps,' she said slowly, 'I'm to blame for that. I mean, I may have flung down the gauntlet a bit.'

'As in issuing a challenge—unwittingly, of course?' he suggested dryly.

'Damien…' She thought for a moment, then she said stubbornly, 'Putting on an act in public is one thing.' She looked out of the window to stare at the flat green fields of sugar cane now flying past. 'Letting it flow into our private times is another.'

'Lee,' he returned flatly, 'it's there. I'm with you in that it's probably not a good idea—I was thinking that this morning, as a matter of fact—but it's already happened.'

Her lips parted soundlessly. Then she swallowed. 'Are you

saying you now find me a bit more interesting than the kitchen sink?'

He looked amused. 'I always found you more interesting than the kitchen sink. To be honest, I found it quite refreshing that *you* found *me* no more interesting than the kitchen sink, but I can't help knowing that is no longer the case.' He turned his head to study her comprehensively then, as she blushed scarlet, switched his dark gaze back to the road with a shrug that said eloquently—*I rest my case.*

When she could recover a sliver of composure, she said unevenly, though she'd hoped to be airy, 'Of course, there are degrees beyond the kitchen sink. It's still a long way to the bedroom—they probably couldn't be further apart, speaking metaphorically.'

They came to the intersection of Ross Lane and the Byron Bay/Ballina road. Damien cruised to a stop and waited for the traffic. Then he turned left as he said, 'On the other hand—' he glanced pointedly down at her legs '—when you're married, there's little distance at all between the bedroom and the kitchen.'

'No!' she said with some force. 'Not in my house—'

'Our house.'

'Not there either. I may rush in where angels fear to tread at times, but you only need eyes in your head to know that I'd be joining a very long queue of women you've discarded, Damien!'

His lips twisted. 'My mother is prejudiced, and her version of this long queue is coloured by the fact that she's dying to have grandchildren—if that's what you're basing this on.'

'It wasn't only your mother! It's your spare bedroom as well.'

'My…?' He looked at her uncomprehendingly, then enlightenment began to dawn.

'I know it's none of my business,' Lee said stiffly, wishing to heaven she could learn to guard her tongue, 'but—'

'You mean the clothes and stuff in there?' he queried gravely.

She nodded. 'Does she know you're married now?' she asked with irony.

'No, she doesn't. Well, unless our beloved mother has passed on the news. But I haven't heard anything from her, so I guess not. She could be away, though.'

'It doesn't matter where she is—' Lee stopped short. '*Our* beloved mother?'

He started to laugh at her expression. 'Yes. All that gear belongs to my sister Melinda. She lives in Cairns but she often comes down to Brisbane for conferences. She manages the Cairns branch of a department store chain. And since the ancestral home was shut up while our parent was overseas, Melinda used my apartment and kept a set of clothes there. That's all.'

'I beg your pardon,' Lee said in deeply mortified tones.

He didn't comment for a moment, then, with a lurking smile, 'If you'd mentioned it at the time I could have saved you some ...discomfort, Lee.'

There was absolutely nothing Lee could find to say to this.

'Here we are.' He nosed the car into a parking spot beneath the famous hoop pines of Byron Bay.

Lee blinked. Such had been her embarrassment she hadn't noticed they were driving through Byron Bay.

Damien switched off. 'I thought we'd get the office bit out of the way first, then have a swim and lunch. OK with you?'

'Uh...fine. Yes, that's fine.'

'Good,' he said gravely. 'There's no need to look so shell-shocked.'

She stared back at him in the close confines of the Porsche and licked her lips uncertainly. He smiled briefly and touched a fingertip to her mouth. 'Let's go.'

The office Damien was leasing was upstairs in a two-storeyed building on the main street. The entry was through a shop-

ping mall. The building was modern, but the previous oc-
cupiers of the suite of offices had gone for a peach-pink decor
throughout that in no way resembled the hallowed halls of
Moore & Moore in Brisbane.

The interior decorator was there to meet them, a striking
but languorous-looking brunette in her early thirties. She lost
a lot of her languor when Damien introduced himself, however, and flicked Lee a look of surprise when she was introduced as Damien's wife. She then proceeded to ignore Lee
completely as she presented Damien with sketches of her
vision for his new branch office.

At first Lee, still grappling with the embarrassing blunder
she'd made and all the revelations of the morning, was too
distracted to care about being ignored. Then she took offence.

'If you ask me, we're going a bit overboard, don't you
think, darling?' She picked up a sketch board and studied it.
'I know Byron is a seaside town, but this looks like the inside
of an aquarium. And this one...' She stared at an austere
black and white decor, even down to a black and white tiled
floor. 'This reminds me of a bathroom or a railway station.'

Damien eyed her narrowly for a moment, then he said
blandly, 'What do you suggest, my love?'

'Off-white walls, terracotta tiles—and if you want some
local flavour there's a factory right here in Byron that pro-
duces stunning woodwork, so you could have the counter in
the reception area custom-made for you with a lovely curved
top. Uh...' She looked around. 'A couple of terracotta leather
Barcelona couches—they're so practical, but spare and elegant—and...' she pointed to a corner '...a display of potted
palms. I could do that for you. Simple, but classy!'

'Mrs Moore—' the interior decorator began, but Damien
cut her off.

'I think my wife is more in tune with my ideas. Thank
you for your time.'

*   *   *

'Wow!' Lee said as they walked towards the beach. 'If looks could kill I'd be six feet under by now. But thank you for your support, Mr Moore.'

'It's the least I could do,' he said wryly. 'But you do realise you've got yourself another job? I like the sound of it very much, by the way, although I have no idea what a Barcelona couch is.'

They stopped in the park above the beach. 'Oh.' Lee's hand flew to her mouth then she turned to Damien urgently. 'There's no way I could design a whole set of offices. I mean colour schemes and the reception area are one thing, but the rest of it—'

'Don't worry about the rest of it. I can get an office equipment design firm to handle desks, storage, filing systems, et cetera. If you can supply the simple classiness you described, that's all I need. Of course there would be a fee involved as well.'

Lee took a deep breath, then shook her head. 'Let me think about it.'

'What's to think?' He took her hand.

She looked up at him and blinked several times. 'All sorts of things,' she said barely audibly. 'So much so that what I really need now is a swim, then lunch.'

He kissed her knuckles. 'All right.'

'That was divine!' Lee said half an hour later as she came out of the water. The surf had been gentle but refreshing, and it was a glorious beach.

They reached their towels and Lee picked hers up and started to dry her hair. 'I don't know why I don't come here more often,' she said whimsically.

Damien grimaced. 'Too busy?' he suggested.

'Well...' Lee spread her towel on the sand and sat down. 'The harder I work, the better it is for your investment in the place.'

'True,' he agreed, and sat down beside her. 'You're very responsible and mature in some ways, Lee.'

She knew she shouldn't ask it, but she couldn't help herself. 'What areas am I *not* responsible and mature in?'

He let his dark gaze flicker over that surprisingly delicious body, made more so at the moment by being sleek and wet and scantily clad.

But just as Lee was anticipating some remark on her appearance, and starting to feel embarrassed about the reactions that dark gaze was evoking in her—a goosebump-reaction that was rather lovely coupled with a sincere appreciation of his powerful physique—he spoke.

'You can be impetuous.'

She relaxed a little. 'I'm told I take after my mother and grandfather in that respect. But I generally act out of the best and purest motives.'

He raised an eyebrow and looked amused. 'Doesn't stop you from getting into trouble from time to time, I imagine.'

Lee looked at him. He'd stretched out on his towel and had his head propped on his elbow. In navy board shorts, he was dark, and divinely proportioned, and just to look at him gave her a strange feeling at the pit of her stomach. She closed her eyes, then reached for her glasses and put them on. 'True,' she agreed judiciously. *And never more so than in relation to yourself, Damien Moore,* she felt like adding, but restrained herself.

She realised suddenly that it was just too much for her to be exposed to him like this—or to have him exposed to her… Whatever, she thought a little wildly, and jumped up to pull her dress from her bag and draw it over her head. 'I'm starving,' she said humorously as she struggled with the dress. 'And I can be quite dangerously impetuous when I'm hungry.'

He sat up. 'As in?'

'As in needing to eat a horse!'

He laughed, stood up with a powerful but easy grace and pulled her dress down for her. 'Or…doing something else altogether?'

Her glasses were down around her chin and she felt she was in utter disarray. Not only because of her tangled hair and glasses, but because he had obviously divined her state of mind. She could see it in the wickedness of his falsely grave look as he smoothed her dress and positioned her glasses on top of her head.

'However,' he continued, 'let's concentrate on soothing the savage breast with some food. I, as it happens, am...starving too.'

He turned away as she grappled with all the innuendoes, to pull his shorts and shirt on. She was still frowning when he turned back, and standing stock still as if frozen to the beach.

'Lee,' he said lightly, and took her hand. Then he paused, as if at some source of inner amusement, and said only, 'Let's go.'

They found a table at the Beach Hotel, on the terrace beneath an umbrella, and ordered lunch. She was sipping a long, cool drink and he had a beer, which he raised in salute to the beach and the ocean. 'Byron at its best. You know, I didn't realise that woman was ignoring you.'

She grinned. 'The interior decorator? That's because you're not used to thinking of me as your wife.'

'True.' He drank some beer. 'I also didn't realise you had opinions in the matter.'

'Neither did I,' Lee confessed. 'I guess it was a combination of being so comprehensively dismissed not only as a fitting partner for you but also as someone who had no taste that got me going.'

He looked humorous. 'Perhaps I should advise people that my wife can be a tiger under certain circumstances.'

Lee laughed. 'Can I really?'

He sat back. 'Cosmo seems to be the only person you have a problem with.'

Before Lee could answer, the electronic paging device telling them their meal was ready buzzed, and Damien got up to collect it.

It wasn't until Lee was halfway through her delicious grilled swordfish, chips and salad that they took up the threads of their conversation. 'I do have a problem with Cosmo,' she admitted. 'He not only gives me the creeps, I'm sure he's dangerous. Has he…what's the term?…filed a suit against us?'

'No. He could be assessing this latest development, though.'

Lee shivered.

But Damien smiled coolly. 'In one way I hope he proceeds, although I doubt he will, just for the pleasure of instructing someone exactly how to demolish him. He may think he can frighten you into wanting to give Plover Park back, but he doesn't frighten me in the slightest.' For a moment he looked so thoroughly authoritative and tough Lee's eyes widened.

'I believe you,' she said quietly. 'I'm only happy I'm not on the other side of a court to you. But what if he has proof that Cyril promised him Plover Park?'

'If he had I'm sure he would have proceeded immediately.'

Lee ate in silence for a while. 'He looked a lot like Cyril, you know, but he's obviously a different kettle of fish altogether.'

Something sharpened in Damien's gaze, but he didn't explain it. Then the tough, dangerous lawyer receded and his lips twisted. 'Are we any nearer to the bedroom from the kitchen?'

She picked up her knife and fork and started to eat again. 'You must see… I mean that woman this morning alone… I don't want to start anything I might regret,' she said disjointedly.

'OK.' He finished his lunch tranquilly and pushed the plate away.

Lee regarded him frustratedly for a long moment.

He fielded her regard with casual unconcern, then grinned ickedly. 'Was that not the response you hoped for, Lee?'

'There are times when you can be incomprehensible and kasperating,' she told him, annoyed.

'There are times when I can be just the opposite.'

Comprehension came to Lee slowly as his dark gaze rifted down her body in the short pink dress. Then she unerstood exactly what he meant as her nerve-endings started tingle and once again her body came alive with a longing be in some private place with him. To be unclothed and uressed and made love to...

This was war, she thought chaotically. How could he do is? How could he tell her it was not a good idea then do is to her? Or—was it a test? What had he said about her ck of interest being refreshing? If only he knew, she rected with some agony.

She swallowed and looked away. Then she suddenly reembered his tiger remark, and she looked back at him with ryly raised eyebrows. 'If you want war, Damien, war is hat you've got.'

CHAPTER SIX

FAMOUS last words, Lee mused a week later.

Far from war, peace had reigned at Plover Park. She' girded her loins, she thought with a spark of black amuse ment, only to have nothing to 'gird' against. She'd gone in tiger mode but the opposition had been playful, helpful— even brotherly—leaving her with a considerable dilemma c her hands. She did not appreciate being treated like a k sister but at the same time she was ready to scratch his ey out should he treat her any other way.

It actually caused her to brood that she might be a litt mad. It was only the strong suspicion he was toying with he that convinced her she was sane.

However, there were other less distressing aspects of th Plover Park Peace, as she thought of it. Damien had provide her with an awful lot of help. He didn't seem to mind work ing in the nursery and he'd even suggested that Bill and Ma might like to take a week off—they'd acquiesced gratefull He'd slashed the paddocks and fixed fences. He'd cleared patch of lantana along the creek bank. He had an enormor amount of energy and his stint as a jackeroo had clearly pr vided him with plenty of skills outside the area of the law

They'd gone through her books together too, and he complimented her on the profits she was showing.

Then there was the way they shared the house. They er joyed a lot of the same television shows, they enjoyed t walk they always took after dinner with Peach, they ha worked well together and they worked out a system of wh would cook when. He kept his wing clear and tidy—he w a pleasant housemate, in other words.

And together they had extended the chicken house, whe

oth Hattie and Shirley became broody. He'd also brought
down an extensive collection of CDs, so there was often music in the background—all kinds, as he had eclectic tastes.
To his amusement Lydia took to following him around and
developed a taste for Mozart.

It was at night, when she often had difficulty sleeping, that
Lee found it hard to resist her subconscious thoughts. Of
course they weren't subconscious in the true sense; they were
thoughts she fought valiantly not to think. Because it *was*
true to say she was falling more and more under the spell of
Damien Moore...

He was a pleasure to watch when he was working. In fact
he often took her breath away. Things she had to labour over
nightily were a piece of cake to him, and it was obvious that
despite being a deskbound lawyer for a lot of his life he was
very fit.

It could be said, she mused one moonlit night, as she stared
over the silvery paddocks when she should have been asleep,
that she was becoming preoccupied with the magnificence of
his body and his easy strength, but it was so much more. She
saw his sense of humour, she shared the things that interested
him, she was coming to know an awful lot about him.

They never lacked things to talk about over meals, at work
or in the evening when they relaxed, often outside on the
terrace as the magnificent summer weather favoured them.
She discovered that he co-owned six racehorses, for example,
and was a breeder in his own right. He showed her pictures
of his mares and the current crop of foals, which she found
fascinating. She even suggested names for the ones he intended to race himself. He told her he had acquired a helicopter licence when he was jackerooing and loved to fly but
never had the time.

Then there was golf. To her amusement, he constructed a
driving range on the farm, with the aid of the tractor, the
mower and the slasher, and a putting green on the lawn. Each
evening he hit dozens of balls and practised his putting. Lee

and Peach watched most evenings, and blinked at his master
of the little white ball. And Lee often chuckled at his expression of disgust at what she would have thought was
tremendous drive.

'The man is a perfectionist,' she often told Peach. 'Don'
mess with him!'

But the most interesting conversations they had were generally over dinner. In light of his culinary expertise, Lee ha
set out to prove herself when it was her turn to cook, wit
the result that the evening meal at Plover Park became a
elegant, delicious affair compared to the plain often hurrie
meals she was used to having on her own. She even took t
using the good china and linen. And there was one thing sh
could do better than he, she discovered. Thanks to inheritin
a gene from her grandmother, she made the lightest, melt-ir
the-mouth pastry.

She turned this art into producing pizza, some filo pastr
parcels with spinach and cheese, a steak and kidney pie
which earned his highest approbation, and an apple pie tha
he made her promise she would cook at least once a week

So they talked food and wine over dinner, and swappe
their experiences of international cuisine. She told him abou
the six months she'd spent backpacking around Europe an
some of the marvellous gardens she'd seen. She told him
lot more, in fact, about her life as an only child and then a
orphan, and how much her adored grandparents had done fc
her.

In return she gained some insights into his life and som
of the things that drove him. There had, she gauged, bee
plenty of pressure to succeed. His grandfather had founde
Moore & Moore, so there was the name to carry on. And c
course there was his mother's position. But there was also
she saw, a genuine fascination for him in the intricacies c
the legal system as well as the law-making process.

It was over the decoration of his offices that the amnest
fell apart.

A week after their lunch at Byron Bay, Lee presented him with her final ideas. She'd got carpet samples, tile samples and paint charts. She'd taken him to the furniture factory, where they'd ordered not only a custom-made counter for the reception area but a couple of unique wood-framed mirrors and a hat and umbrella stand. She'd tracked down a distributor of Barcelona couches and put Damien in touch with a couple of local artists whose work, she felt, would be worthy of hanging on the walls of Moore & Moore. And she'd found a couple of lovely pottery urns for the palms she'd suggested.

She laid the paint charts and samples out on the dining room table and explained her preferences to him. She also gave him a fair estimation of the costs involved.

'Barcelona couches don't come cheap,' she finished ruefully. 'But they are nice.' She handed him an illustration.

He studied it thoughtfully, then her equally as thoughtfully. She'd just come home from doing the weekly shopping and wore a three-quarter-length green and white dotted sleeveless dress. Her hair was loose, the colour of polished mahogany, and her freckles were noticeable.

'Too expensive?' she asked at last, with some anxiety in her green eyes.

'Not at all. You generally have to pay for class. Is that a new dress?'

'Uh…why do you ask?'

His lips quirked. 'I've never seen it before, that's all.'

'It's so old I can't remember how old it is,' she said wryly. 'I don't wear a lot of dresses, and the last new one I had was—well, come to think of it there are two, and not that long ago.'

'Would one of them be a little black number by any chance?' he asked with a glint of amusement.

'Yes,' she conceded. 'Which I'll probably never wear again.'

'That would be a pity.' He took in her uncertain expression and smiled inwardly. 'This one also suits you, though.' He turned back to the dining room table. 'And all of this suit me—so...' he pulled a piece of paper from his pocket and handed it to her... 'this is for you.'

She unfolded what turned out to be a cheque and gasped at the amount. 'Oh! No! I mean I couldn't possibly accept this. Thank you very much.' She went to give it back to him. 'But I don't want any payment at all.'

He shoved his hands in the pockets of his jeans so she was left with the cheque, 'Lee, don't be silly.'

'I'm not being silly,' she protested. 'I couldn't possibly pay *you* for all the work you've done around here, so I don't expect to be paid for anything either, and...and...' She paused and thought frantically. 'It would be far too much even if I did.'

'It's what I would have paid an interior decorator,' he said.

'Maybe, but all I've done is get some samples!'

'Listen to me, Lee,' he said, in a way that told her he'd gone into lawyer mode and she was going to have to fight every inch of the way to *get* her way, 'it's not all you did. Anyone can assemble paints and samples, but it's *ideas* interior decorators charge a small fortune for. I happen to think your ideas are brilliant, so I'm happy to pay for them.'

'I still don't want it.' Her nose fined down and she eyed him defiantly. 'I don't need charity and that's what this smacks of.'

'For crying out loud, Lee,' he said through his teeth, 'it is not charity! Nor is it me personally paying you. It comes out of the budget the firm allocated to the new branch, and I can assure you it's well within budget and perfectly legitimate.'

She disagreed. 'How can it be? I'm a gardener, not an interior decorator!'

'Didn't you tell me you'd taken some courses? Don't you have any faith in your ideas?' he shot back.

She blinked. 'Of course I do. That is—'

'Don't you *design* gardens, and did you not tell me you

Lennox Head commission has been broadened into the design of an indoor pool room?'

'Yes, but—'

'Then you're legitimate, Lee,' he said coolly.

'There's a difference between a pool room and a suite of offices!'

'There's not,' he disagreed. 'It's a matter of taste and discrimination, of which you obviously have plenty. Once the branch is finished, I wouldn't be surprised if we get plenty of enquiries about who the decorator was. As for your argument about what I've done here—there is no argument. I own half this place, so any work I do is in my own interest.'

'I don't—'

'Moreover,' he interrupted grimly, 'if you persist with this nonsense, I'll do what you've been dying for me to do all week...' He paused and looked humorous for a moment, 'Something I've had a bit of trouble with myself.' He shrugged. 'There's no other way to win an argument with you, anyway.'

'I don't know what you're talking about!'

'This, Lee,' he supplied, and pulled her into his arms. 'This,' he added barely audibly, and started to kiss her.

'No,' she breathed, but the feel of being in his encircling arms was intoxicating; it *was*, perversely, what she had wanted all week—although she'd fought so hard to stop herself from thinking about it. Not that she'd expected quite this, she thought confusedly. His mouth hard and demanding against hers, his body the same, intensely masculine and hungry. But conversely, after the first shock of it, her own hunger became demanding and allowed her to be carried away. As if she were flowering in his arms, as if she was the flame that had lit his ardour. It was a unique feeling.

'So,' he said when they pulled apart at last, 'it was mutual.'

She laid her forehead against his chest, her breathing still

ragged, her senses on fire. 'Of course it was mutual. I don't
go around kissing men I don't want to kiss like that.'

She felt his chest jolt and knew he was laughing at her.
She raised her green eyes to his. 'Perhaps I should qualify
that—'

'No. Don't. It was pure Lee Westwood.'

'Then perhaps I should say this, Damien. Have you fallen
in love with me?'

'I might have known you'd need to give it a name, Lee.'

She froze. He felt it, and after a moment tilted her chin so
he could see her eyes, wide and stunned before she swiftly
lowered her lashes.

'Lee,' he said quietly, 'I didn't mean to make fun of you.'

'No. It's not that. I mean…' She tailed off confusedly.

'Let's look at this from another point of view,' he said
then. 'Have *you* fallen in love with *me*?'

Her lashes rose, and for one mad moment she was tempted
to say…*I thought I had months ago, little to know that what
I felt then was nothing compared to now.* But where to go?
Where to hide once she'd made that admission and found it
wasn't reciprocated? 'I don't…know,' she said barely audibly. 'I…it's happened to me a couple of times before, so—'
She broke off awkwardly.

'An attraction to a man who didn't turn out to be the love
of your life?' he suggested.

'Yes,' she agreed, although the truth of the matter was that
her two previous encounters with what she'd thought was
love had been pale imitations of what she felt for Damien
Moore, what he did to her.

He smoothed her loose hair and smiled absently into her
eyes. 'Then could you believe that I'm in the same boat?'

'Oh, yes, easily!' Lee heard herself say, and flinched inwardly. What was she? she wondered. Her own devil's advocate? 'If anything I'm sure men have more of a problem
with it than women—especially men like you.' This time she
flinched openly as his eyebrows shot up.

'I'll leave that unanswered for the moment,' he said rather dryly, 'in favour of another question. What do you suggest we do about it?'

A tangle of thoughts flew through Lee's head. 'You... kissed me,' she said cautiously at last.

He grimaced. 'Out of exasperation. But,' he added, 'it was something I had been thinking of all week.'

'Something you wouldn't have done if I hadn't frustrated the life out of you, though?' she asked.

He hesitated briefly. 'No, Lee.'

She pushed herself away from him and walked over to stare out of the terrace doors. 'I'll have to take care I don't frustrate you again,' she said in a cool little voice. Then she turned and faced him. 'Damien, there are enough complications in our lives already. An affair—'

'We are married, Lee,' he broke in.

'Not really,' she denied. 'We both know that at the end of the twelve months we'll go our separate ways, so it would be an affair and therefore a complication we don't need.'

'What if we find out that Cyril was right?' He looked at her intently.

'He wasn't,' she said steadily. 'I'm not the right girl for you, Damien.' A small smile lit her eyes, although inside she felt far from smiling. 'You've been wonderful down here, better than I ever dreamt you could be, but it's only an interlude for you—a break and a bit of a novelty.' She looked at him questioningly.

'Perhaps,' he conceded after a moment.

'Whereas this is my kind of lifestyle, even if it isn't at Plover Park, so there's a real chasm between us in that direction, and the other thing is—I suspect *I'm* a bit of a novelty for you as well.'

His lips twisted. 'My one-woman SWAT team wife? Perhaps,' he said again. 'Though I didn't feel as if I was kissing a SWAT team.' He paused. 'This chasm you talk about—different lifestyles may not be such a bar to a successful marriage.'

Lee blinked several times as she cast around for comprehension.

'But,' he continued before she could speak, 'if that's how you feel, Lee, I…bow to your wisdom.'

'Thank you,' she said, and at the same time she wondered whether the pain that had gathered around her heart would ever go away.

'On the other hand—' Damien bent to pick up the cheque that had fluttered to the floor during their embrace '—I don't want any arguments about this.' He put it into her hand and closed her fingers over it. 'Just do as you're told and deposit it in your bank, Lee.'

'I…' She gathered herself, as if to take issue with him.

But he said gravely, 'Don't forget what the consequences could be.'

'You wouldn't…?'

He smiled fleetingly. 'I'm a man, remember? You yourself told me only minutes ago how much worse these kind of things are for men to handle.'

Not sure if he was serious, not at all sure that her observation hadn't been trite in the first place, Lee started to colour, and knew she looked confused and possibly even juvenile.

So it was no surprise when he started to laugh, but still bitter fruit for her to swallow—and there was worse to come. He stopped laughing, but his eyes were still alive with amusement as he patted her on the head. 'OK, let's call it quits. In view of this development, I think I might go back to Brisbane for a couple of days. As a matter of fact something has come up, and I was thinking of doing it anyway. But I'll need to come back to tie up all the Byron Bay ends.'

She could think of absolutely nothing to say as a vista of Plover Park and her life there without him filled her mind's eye—not a sunlight vista, but a cold and lonely one...

'Lee?'

She blinked and refocused, to see that all the amusement had drained from his expression. Just don't let him be able to read my mind, she prayed. 'Um...yes—no, that's fine,' she said disjointedly. 'Is it anything serious? Whatever it is that's come up?' she queried.

He hesitated, his eyes narrow and very probing. Then he said, 'A very important client of mine has got himself into a spot of bother, that's all.'

'Oh. When will you go?'

'Are your grandparents back?'

'Yes. Nan rang earlier. She asked us to dinner, as a matter of fact.'

'You go,' he said quietly, and glanced at his watch. 'I can be back in Brisbane in time for dinner.'

Her eyes widened.

'It's for the best, Lee. And I will be back; I'm just not sure when. My client has complicated matters by being in Vanuatu.'

'Really? Oh, well, definitely—I mean, it's for the best, I'm sure!' She forcibly stirred herself into action. 'Will I go ahead and order all this?' She gestured towards the dining room table.

'If you wouldn't mind. I plan to open the branch four weeks from today, so anything you order has to be installed by then.' He paused and frowned. 'Look, I can take it with me and get someone from the Brisbane office to do all that—'

'No way, José!' Lee said. She opened her hand and smoothed out the cheque she was still clutching. 'If I'm being paid this amount of money, I intend to earn it.'

'Lee, it may mean many trips to Byron Bay that you wouldn't normally make—'

'Damien,' she said with the light of battle in her eyes, 'you can do your damnedest, you can kiss me out of *exasperation* until the cows come home, but this is one argument I intend to win!'

His lips twisted and something she couldn't read came into his eyes as he studied her from head to toe in her pretty dress, her straight spine, her militant expression. Then he murmured, 'I believe you this time. Never let it be said that I don't recognise tiger mode when I see it.'

She couldn't help relaxing and looking rueful.

'That's better,' he said softly. 'But just remember, you're *not* a one-woman SWAT team, so no dicing with death on your own while I'm away.'

'OK.'

He seemed about to say something, but Lee turned away as the phone rang.

Half an hour later, when he was ready to leave, she was able to be friendly and casual. But she stood staring after the blue Porsche for a long time. Then she breathed deeply and said to Lydia, 'I'm sure I did the right thing. If it's hard now, how much harder would it be after I'd slept with him?'

Lydia stood on tiptoe, stretched his wings, and subsided rather mournfully.

He was to be away for four days.

During that time Lee barely stopped to eat and sleep. Hard work seemed to be the only antidote for the crippling feeling of loss that plagued her. Hard work seemed to be the only way to still the circles of her mind.

But really there was only one way to look at it, she thought wearily that first night as she tossed in bed. She had presented him with a simple equation: they were not right for each other and they could only complicate their lives—unbearably for her, did he but know it—if they gave in to the attraction between them. And Damien had conceded the wisdom of it.

What that meant—and she couldn't fail to grasp it—was that she could never be more than a passing affair to him. Perhaps if the real Lee Westwood was the kind of girl he'd taken to Ella Patroni's party, rather than a one-woman SWAT team who wasn't content unless she was growing things, she might have stood a chance...

She stilled on the thought. Did she honestly believe she wasn't his type? Didn't that imply that she *knew* what his type of woman was—but how? She'd never met any of his lovers...so how could she be so sure she wouldn't be right for him? she thought suddenly.

It was four o'clock in the morning and a huge moon was setting to the west, casting an eerie light over the garden and lightening the outlines of her bedroom—she never closed her curtains because she loved to wake up to the sunrise, and the main bedroom at Plover Park had windows to the east and west.

She turned over and heard Peach stir in his basket outside the sliding veranda door. Shortly Henry would start crowing and the bird and animal kingdom would wake to greet a fresh new day. Not that long ago she would have bounced out of bed to grasp that fresh new day, but that was before Damien Moore had got into her blood and her heart.

The funny thing was, she mused, she knew so much more about him now—except, perhaps, for the vital element: what he was looking for in a soul mate.

Something his mother had said surfaced in her mind. *I sometimes wonder if Damien isn't quite content the way he is. Too many women have made fools of themselves over him. In fact a marriage of convenience might suit him admirably...*

Lee stirred restlessly and sat up. Her response at the time had been to ask his mother why she thought that. Evelyn Moore had shrugged and said that properly set up, with both partners suffering no illusions, a marriage of convenience had been known to work—and anyway, the falling-in-love kind of marriage carried no guarantees of success, as she saw only too often in her court.

'But what puts a man into that kind of mind-set?' Lee had posed.

Evelyn had looked at her rather cynically out of Damien's dark eyes and commented that monogamy was harder for men than women, that a primarily business arrangement which nevertheless ensured heirs and order was perhaps not to be sneezed at from a male point of view.

Lee had stared at her open-mouthed, and—possibly because she had felt sudden embarrassment about associating her only son with this kind of male mind-set—Damien's mother had then said rather abruptly that she was only theorising in general and obviously this marriage was a different thing entirely.

Now, sitting up in bed with her head in her hands, Lee had to wonder if his mother hadn't been more right than she knew. Not about Damien's marriage to her, but could her own mysterious certainty that she wasn't the right person for him come from an instinct that this *was* his mind-set after too many women had made fools of themselves over him?

It would explain a lot, she felt. And she was suddenly certain that if she had ever let her defences slip, let him know in any way how she'd felt about him up until Cyril's will was contested, he would no more have suggested they get married than fly to the moon.

But was the awful irony of it the fact that their marriage of convenience was starting to look more attractive to him? Was that what his remark had been about—the remark she hadn't understood at the time? *Different lifestyles may not be a bar to a successful marriage...*

She lifted her head and knew with a cold, sinking certainty that she could not survive the kind of marriage his mother had outlined to Damien Moore. Two separate individuals who came together only to ensure heirs and order but lived different lifestyles at other times...

No, don't even contemplate it, Lee, she told herself. Even

if it means losing Plover Park you need somehow to place yourself away from this kind of close contact with him.

But how? she wondered, and rubbed her face.

Three days later she hadn't come up with an answer. In the meantime, the weather had broken, some much-needed rain had fallen and the temperature had dropped. Then fate intervened.

She took Peach for a walk after dinner. It was a cool evening, and wet underfoot although it wasn't raining. They went up to the shed to close up the chicken house for the night, then crossed the paddock to stroll along the creek and inspect the Murray Greys, who were grazing contentedly along the banks. 'All present and correct!' she said to Peach. 'The creek's up a bit. OK—let's go home.'

It was quite dark by then, so she flicked on her torch for the walk back to the house—and nearly died to see a large snake right in front of her.

She stepped backwards instinctively, slipped in the mud and fell into the creek. The shock of it took her breath away and she flailed around, slipping on the mossy rocks, getting soaked. Then one foot slid between two rocks and she couldn't free it—and Peach was barking hysterically at the snake.

'Leave it alone, Peach,' she screamed. 'It may be only a carpet snake but it could be a brown. Please, Peach,' she begged. She cast around for the torch but couldn't find it, then tugged desperately at her ankle but nothing happened.

'Damn and frustration! This can't be happening to me,' she sobbed. But it was. For the next hour she was forced to sit on her bottom with creek water swirling up to her chest as she tried in vain to release her foot. She called for Peach, who came back to her repeatedly but only to lick her face before resuming his guardian role of keeping himself between her and the snake.

Her only consolation was that the snake must have started to move away, because Peach's barking got further away and it took him longer to come back to her. Then it started to rain and she started to get cold.

Just as she'd tearfully decided she was going to have to spend the night in the creek, she saw a light bobbing across the paddock and heard someone calling her name. Damien.

It was Peach who led him to her, and as the light of his torch flickered over her he swore. 'What the bloody hell have you been doing, Lee?' he barked. 'I thought I told you not to—'

He stopped abruptly, and then he was down on his knees beside her. 'Sorry. What happened? When there was no one in the house and I could hear Peach barking I... What happened?' He put his arms around her.

She sobbed out the whole comedy of errors into his shoulder and then couldn't stop crying. 'I *hate* snakes,' she wept and shuddered.

'Lee,' he said gently, 'you poor darling.' And he hugged her until the storm of weeping subsided. 'OK. Let me see if I can free you now.'

He pulled a hanky from his pocket. It was wet, but she could at least blow her nose. 'Tell me if I'm hurting you,' he warned. Nothing he did released her foot, and he finally said, 'Lee, I'm going to have get a crowbar. I'll be as quick as I can. Look—' He ripped off his tie—he was as muddy and wet as she was—grabbed Peach and attached the tie to the dog's collar. 'Now he can stay right here with you to protect you. OK?'

She shuddered again, then nodded and buried her face in Peach's fur. Damien stood up, studied her for a moment, then did a quick sweep of the bank. There was no sign of the snake. 'I'll be back before you know it, Lee.'

'OK,' she mumbled with her teeth chattering. 'I'm OK. I may not look it now, but I am.'

'That's my girl!' He came back into the water and planted a quick kiss on the top of her head.

He was no more than ten minutes and came back on the tractor. In only a few minutes more, with the tractor headlights bathing the scene, he'd moved one of the deeply embedded rocks and released her foot. Then he carried her to the bank and eased her boot off. Finally, after some manipulation, he said. 'Not broken—a bit swollen, maybe a slight sprain. What do you think? Could you stand?'

She did so cautiously, with his help, and although her ankle was sore it was up to bearing her weight.

'Good.' He pulled a blanket out of a plastic bag and wrapped her up in it. 'Can you hang on if I put you on the carry-all?'

She nodded, but her teeth were still chattering. All the same, she said, 'I've...r-r-ruined...you. Sorry!'

He looked down at himself, formally dressed in grey trousers and a cream silk shirt, although minus his jacket and tie, and glinted a smile at her. 'Who cares? OK, hang on—this is the last lap.'

The first thing he did when he got her into the house was administer a tot of brandy.

'Now to get you warm,' he said as he carried her into the bedroom. 'How long were you there before I arrived?'

'I don't know. About an hour, I think. The trouble is I *hate* snakes. They can swim, you know.' She was speechless for a moment, then, 'That's why I was less than my best—and I was petrified Peach would get bitten—what are you doing?'

Damien continued what he was doing, which was taking her out of her sodden clothes. 'Getting you warm. Don't worry about it.' He went on conversationally, 'Not to mention in your list of woes being soaked, with the creek rising, by the look of it, and catching pneumonia. But I know how you feel. I hate snakes too.'

Lee blinked at him through some dripping strands of hair. 'I thought you said you could take them or leave them?'

He pulled her jeans down to her ankles. 'Step out of them if you can.'

'I…' Lee hesitated and then did as she was bid, which left her in her bra and panties. 'I…'

'I think I said I didn't like them.' He picked her up before she could finish speaking and carried her into the bathroom. 'But it would be more accurate to say I loathe them.' He set her on her feet, deftly released her bra and slid her panties down, then switched the shower on. While she was still trying to cover herself up he lifted her into the cubicle beneath a spray of blessedly warm water.

She gasped, but it was wonderful and she closed her eyes for a moment. Then her lashes flew up and she saw he was still there. 'Damien—'

He interrupted gravely, 'Why don't you reflect on a bit of macho evasion?'

'You mean—over snakes?'

'Yep.' He looked wickedly amused and picked up her hand to rest it on the stainless steel bar installed on the shower wall. 'In the meantime, hang on to this if you feel wonky. I'll go and change—I'll only be a minute.'

He came back in five, showered and wearing tracksuit pants and a plaid flannel shirt. Lee was still standing in the shower with a bemused expression on her face, but some warmth was trickling through to her bones at last.

'Had enough?' he queried, and picked up a towel.

What was wrong with her? she wondered. Why wasn't she more flustered? Why hadn't she got out and got dressed rather than standing like a naked statue beneath the stream of warm water until he came back and subjected her to that impersonal dark gaze?

Point one, she thought, that dark gaze was *completely* impersonal—as had been his earlier undressing of her. Point

two, her will even to move and think seemed to be affected
—she might as well be a naked statue. Of course it could be
that she was still in shock, she reflected, but which had been
the greater shock...?

'Lee?' He held the towel open.

'Thanks,' she murmured, and stepped out at last to be en-
folded in it. Not long afterwards she was wearing a nightgown he had pulled from a drawer and slipped over her head,
she was in bed, where he had put her, propped up against
some pillows, and Peach had come to keep her company
while Damien made them something to eat.

'Peach deserves a medal,' he'd said with a lurking smile
before departing for the kitchen.

Now Lee stroked the dog's silky ears and said to him
softly, 'Why do I feel like this, Peach? As if I'm a speck of
dust floating in the wind? He was only doing what anyone
would have in the circumstances—what did I expect? That
he wouldn't be able to control himself, faced with me in my
birthday suit?'

No, she answered herself mentally, of course not. So what
is this feeling I have?

It came to her gradually—she felt like a kid. A kid Damien
Moore was fond of—fond enough to make sure she was all
right and didn't have any ill effects from a nightmare experience, but no more, and it hurt her.

'Lee?'

She looked up with a start as he placed a tray across her
knees. There was a fluffy, fragrant herb omelette, toast and
a glass of wine.

'Thanks, but I don't think I can eat—'

He overrode her. 'Yes, you can. Don't be silly, just do as
you're told. I'll bring mine in and we'll eat together.'

He left and Lee took up her wine, sipped it, and was
amazed at what was going through her mind—especially considering what she'd been through not that long ago. Of course
she wouldn't do it, she mused—she wouldn't get the oppor-

tunity for one thing—but the temptation was almost unbearable.

In the end, though, it was what she'd been through that did it for her...

CHAPTER SEVEN

SHE ate it all.

Damien pulled an armchair up close to the bed and ate his omelette from a tray on his knees. They talked desultorily. He told her he'd only come back for the night, just to check out how she and the new office were doing, because he was off to Vanuatu the next afternoon.

Lee raised her eyebrows. 'He must be a very special client.'

Damien shrugged. 'He's a loveable larrikin, but he's always trying to bend the rules.'

'How long will you be there?'

'A couple of days. How are things going with the office?'

'Good. Painter, carpet-layer and tiler all organised and they should be finished by the end of next week. Then the office furniture people can move in. The only thing that's going to be a tight squeeze is the reception desk, but the cabinet-maker assures me he will get it done, come hell or high water.'

Damien smiled fleetingly. 'You're a clever girl.'

Lee looked around the comfortable lamplit bedroom. The bed was double, with a lovely cherrywood curved bedhead and she was ensconced beneath a cream quilt patterned with tiny roses, leaning against frilled cream pillows. The cream damask curtains, she noticed for the first time, were closed. But that didn't stop her mind from taking a leap to the creek and the awful panic she'd suffered while trapped in it.

'Not so clever a little while ago,' she murmured.

'It could have happened to anyone.' He'd taken their trays away and made coffee. 'However...' He paused and looked at her thoughtfully. 'It is the problem about living here on your own, Lee.'

She finished her coffee and lay back. 'There's not a lot I can do about that.'

'I think you should bite the bullet and move your grandparents in with you.'

She grimaced and combed her fingers through her hair.

'You do love them.'

'I adore them—I'll think about it.'

He stretched his legs out and thought how small she looked. And pale against that wonderful auburn hair. Then he thought of her standing in the shower, looking all dazed but exquisite, with her slender lines, gentle curves and pink satiny skin... He moved restlessly and issued a warning to himself along the lines of—*Don't go down that road, mate. She's right about the complications.*

But there was something about her at the moment that he couldn't put his finger on, he mused.

'You're not...' He paused. 'Not upset with yourself because your one-woman SWAT team didn't come through, or anything ridiculous like that, Lee?'

'No. Damien—how old do you take me for?' she asked ruefully.

'You look about sixteen at the moment,' he commented a little dryly. 'I don't suppose you have anything to help you sleep?'

'Uh—I haven't. But I'll be fine.'

'Sure?' He got up and came to stand beside the bed with a frown in his eyes. 'You've been awfully quiet.'

'I think I'm exhausted,' she replied, and discovered it was true as she couldn't help yawning.

'All right. See if you can sleep. I've got some work to do so I'll be around for a while; I'm only down the passage. Goodnight, Lee.' He switched off the bedside lamp and laid his hand briefly against her cheek. 'Sleep well.'

'Goodnight, Damien, thanks for everything,' she said drowsily.

And she did fall asleep, but only for a couple of hours.

Then she woke up and she was back in the creek, trapped, freezing and scared of drowning, imagining a snake swimming towards her. She cast aside the bedclothes and stumbled out of bed, making quite a noise on the polished floor, and as she bumped into the bedside table. Then a strong pair of arms surrounded her and Damien was saying, 'Lee, Lee—you're quite safe! I'm here!'

'Oh, thank heavens!' she breathed. 'Don't let me go, please!'

He hadn't.

He'd taken her back to bed and got in beside her, still fully clothed. And he'd held her and talked to her about anything and everything. Vanuatu—which he knew well, apparently—his father—who had been the kind of man you either loved or hated and the times he hadn't been sure whether he loved or hated him back.

She'd dozed off a couple of times, only to wake with that wrenching jerk, but he had still been there. Then she'd fallen into a deep, dreamless sleep.

It was just daylight when she woke, to find him still there, asleep beside her with his arms wrapped around her.

She tried not to move as the growing light revealed his features to her—less autocratic in sleep than she'd ever seen them, with blue shadows on his jaw. But he woke of his own accord not much later, and blinked at her uncomprehendingly. Then, looking wry, he said, 'Well, Mrs Moore, it's finally come to this! No, just joking.' And he started to release her.

But Lee couldn't let it happen. She slipped her arms around his neck and cuddled up against him.

'Lee.' He moved his chin on the top of her head and his voice was different, serious. 'I think I better get going, otherwise—who knows what might happen?'

'That's fine with me.'

She felt him stiffen, then he was tilting her chin so he could see her eyes. 'What do you mean?'

She didn't attempt to evade his intent, frowning gaze. 'I…need you, Damien. Please stay.'

He went to say something, changed his mind and said instead. 'It's no way to try to block out snakes, creeks and nightmares, Lee.'

'It's not that,' she said calmly. 'It may well pass, but right now I can't think of anything I'd rather be doing, that's all. Besides, I've got something to prove.'

'*All?* What have you got to prove?' he asked.

'That I'm not sixteen,' she said softly.

'Lee—that was— Would you rather I'd taken advantage of you last night?'

'No. You have my permission to take full advantage of me this morning, though.' And she moved against him, offered him her mouth.

Damien stared down at her face, with its freckles, the swathe of wonderful hair, her closed eyes, and he shut his teeth hard. 'I could easily have done this last night,' he said frustratedly. 'You were so lovely, so lost-looking, but…'

Her lashes lifted, a faint smile curved her lips, and a glint of pure essence of Lee Westwood amusement lit her green eyes.

He groaned, hugged the slim, warm length of her to him, and knew he was gone. Which he acknowledged with a wry twisting of his lips before he started to kiss her.

While it was warm and amusing to begin with, it soon got completely out of hand… At least, that was what Lee's impression of it was and it caused her to wonder what her expectations had been. To keep it light? But how strange was that? To be so determined to sleep with a man and then try to keep it light?

Not long afterwards she couldn't think about anything but what he was doing to her…

'Let's not rush this,' he said huskily.

'No—I mean—was I rushing?'

He cupped her face, then slid his hands down the column of her throat, flicked open a couple of buttons and spread them across her shoulders beneath her nightgown.

'No. I was directing that warning to myself.'

She looked into his eyes and saw they were quizzical.

'I don't know whether to believe you,' she murmured, and moved as two more buttons were released and his hands covered her breasts.

'You should,' he replied. 'Ever since I tucked a carnation between these I've wondered about them.'

Lee bit her lip and closed her eyes as he started to play with her nipples. A rush of exquisite sensation flowed through her.

'Nice?' he queried.

'Oh, yes…'

'Exceedingly nice for me too, except—'

Her lashes flew up and he laughed softly at her expression.

'Except that I'd like to see what I'm doing, that's all,' he reassured her. 'May I?'

She could only nod and lie quietly beside him once her nightgown was removed. Then not so quietly as he propped his head on his elbow and drew his hand down her body slowly, very gently, and told her what he thought of her figure. 'Such a revelation out of your baggy T-shirts and eternal jeans,' he murmured as that stroking hand moved down. 'You know that black dress you're rather scathing about these days?'

'Mmm.'

'It was the first intimation I got that there was so much sheer class to you.'

'Class?' she whispered.

'Yes. Skin like satin. Perfect little breasts.' He touched them. 'A fascinating bottom and legs—mind you, I did always think you had great legs. Last night in the shower, all rosy from the warm water, you were like a figurine any man would love to own.'

Lee breathed unevenly as his hand circled her hips and the tops of her thighs, then moved away tantalisingly. 'Thank you.' She sat up suddenly. 'But there's only so much more of this I can take.'

He sat up as well, and pulled his shirt and tracksuit pants off. He took her in his arms and she sighed with pleasure, because he felt wonderful, hard and strong, and it was glorious to move against him, to run her hands across the width of his shoulders, to feel her breasts crushed against the wall of his chest. And that was when things began to get thoroughly out of hand...

That was when they explored each other's bodies intimately, until the lovely rhythm of lovemaking enveloped them and there was only one thing left to do—take and be taken. Something he did as he kissed her breasts and teased her nipples with his teeth, so that she arched in his arms, exquisitely mindless with desire.

She thought things had got out of hand before, but their climax was simultaneous, and the sensations that washed through her were so unique she felt as if she'd broken through to some rare upper atmosphere. It took a while for her slim, sweat-soaked body to come down from those incredible heights...

'Well.'

It wasn't a question, and it wasn't quite a statement of surprise that Damien made, but close to both.

Her lashes fluttered up. She was still in his arms and he kissed the tip of her nose. 'What do you mean—well?' she whispered.

He grimaced. 'That was exceedingly...fine.'

'And a bit of a surprise?' she hazarded.

He hesitated. 'Don't take this wrong, but...' His lips twisted, 'You've always been full of surprises, Lee. On the other hand, I got the feeling it had never happened for you before.' His dark eyes were narrow and suddenly probing.

A faint wash of colour rose in her cheeks, but she said honestly, 'It hadn't. Not like that. I had started to wonder if there was something wrong with me, but I've actually had very little experience, so…' She shrugged, then looked impish. 'Either that or I was in the hands of a master.'

He looked fleetingly amused. 'It had not a little to do with your hands, Mrs Moore. So.' He smoothed her hair. 'I think you'd better come to Vanuatu with me, Lee.'

Once again a battle royal continued in the Porsche as it flashed towards Brisbane.

'Still not speaking to me?' he queried.

'I said it all and you took no notice of me. You actually threatened me with violence, Damien,' she said, staring straight ahead.

'All I threatened was that I would bodily put you in the car myself, Lee. Hardly violence.' He glinted her a wicked little look.

'That's a matter of opinion. You…you just took over!' She spread her hands, then clenched them into fists.

'At least you know you don't have to worry about Plover Park. Your grandparents are more than happy to caretake for you for a few days.' He paused significantly. 'They thought a bit of a break was just what you need!'

She said nothing.

'Of course I have to wonder what the root cause of this rebellion is,' he continued reflectively. 'Were you planning to sleep with me just the once, Lee?'

'You're doing it again, Damien. I am not a rebellious teenager! I'm quite entitled to make whatever decisions I make!'

'Only once?' he mused. 'I mean if you're going to do it all—'

'I—it—I just wanted to do it at the time,' she broke in

intensely. 'I haven't thought beyond that yet—I haven't had
the chance!'

He laughed softly. 'More rushing in where angels fear to
tread? Unfortunately, Lee, once may have been enough for
you, but it's not for me.' He looked across at her. 'Not by a
long chalk, my lovely sprite.' He put his hand over her
clenched fists. 'In fact it's just as well we have a plane to
catch, otherwise I'd be tempted to stop at the nearest hotel.'

Lee blinked at him and licked her lips. 'Really?'

His dark eyes played over her and were suddenly deadly
serious. 'You don't know much about men. Really, Lee.'

Two afternoons later on Erakor Island, a few minutes' ferry
ride from Port Vila, the capital of Vanuatu, the setting sun
laid a dancing path of light across the Erakor Lagoon as Lee
watched. The thin crooked stakes of a fish trap stood to attention in the water and a Vanuatan paddled a small outrigger
canoe fashioned from a hollow tree trunk towards the trap.

But as she watched from the veranda of their bungalow,
which was right on the water, the serene scene started to
change. The waves on the inner bar got up and were audible
as the wind changed, or maybe the tide turned. Then the sun
was blanked out by cloud and it began to rain heavily. The
hammering on the roof, straight down kind of rain, that
caused the surface of the water to dimple and spit—rain that
shrouded the view in a curtain of grey and made the air hot
and heavy with humidity.

It didn't last long, slowing to a shower as it swept out to
sea, and the surf was audible again, the colours briefly re-
stored. The setting sun, sinking through charcoal strata cloud
like an old rose-gold ball, swiftly lost its power to make the
water dance along the path of its rays. Dusk crept in.

Lee watched it all entranced. She'd fallen in love with
Erakor Island. It was like a lush tropical park, she'd thought
as she'd first wandered down the broad beaten path beneath

the soaring coconut palms and beside giant liliums. A park with ghosts.

She'd strayed from the path onto the thick smooth turf and come across two graves. Amanda Bruce, missionary and wife of the Reverend J.W. Mackenzie in one, and her three babies in the other. She'd lost the first one on Christmas Day, 1875, at thirteen months, then two more at similar ages over the next twelve years. She had died in 1893.

Tears had come to Lee's eyes as she'd read the inscriptions and she'd wondered if Amanda Bruce had had any surviving children.

Further down the path she'd come to a stone erected in memory of the four Samoans who had first brought the gospel to Erakor. But Erakor was about life too, she'd discovered, while Damien had been closeted in conferences on the mainland with his wayward client and she had been left to her own devices.

The Erakor people had been relocated to the mainland, just across the lagoon, but they worked on the island, at the resort, and were partners in it.

There was an open-air chapel on the island that was still used for weddings, and the relocated village of Erakor, across the water, abounded with life. There was always chatter and laughter floating across the lagoon, and there was a football ground just beyond the beach, where they trained and played. There were often children swimming and diving. And how wonderfully simple to step into an outrigger canoe and paddle your way across the lagoon to work? The Erakor people also fished from their canoes, or snorkelled for shellfish.

Lee had snorkelled herself, and been fascinated by the millions of different coloured starfish that lay on the sandy bottom of the lagoon. She was fascinated by the people, too, with their friendliness and their sense of humour.

From the mainland you could summon the ferry twenty-four hours a day by pushing a button that rang on the island. And from the island, if the ferryman wasn't in sight, there was a gong you hit with a club, beneath a sign that said, 'Sipos yu wantem ferry, yu killem gong'.

And last night, beneath a full moon, a woman in the village had started to sing a song like no other Lee had heard, her voice carrying as clear as a bell in the still, silvery night.

She was thinking of that moon song again now, then heard a sound and turned her head to look into the bungalow to see Damien stretch and sit up. He'd been up most of the night and had worked all morning, so an afternoon nap hadn't seemed such a bad idea—although he'd told her he was a man who never napped, just before he'd fallen fast asleep.

Now, he ran his hands through his hair, looked at his watch and grimaced. 'Sorry—'

'Don't be. I've been quite happy,' she said, and opened her arms wide to embrace the whole experience of Erakor.

'So this wasn't such a bad idea after all, Lee?'

'It was brilliant,' she conceded.

'Come here, then.'

She got up and joined him on the bed.

He took her in his arms and lay back with her. 'My ideas generally are brilliant.' He kissed her throat and slid his hands beneath her blouse.

'Ah. Has it occurred to you how smug that sounds?'

'Smug? Why are you wearing a bra, by the way?'

'I generally do and, yes, smug. Don't change the subject.'

'OK.' He unbuttoned her blouse and took it and her bra off.

'Damien...' She breathed unevenly as he played with her nipples. 'If that's not changing the subject I don't know what is.'

'On the contrary, Lee, it's a subject that is wholly occupying my mind at the moment. Ah, I love it when they do that.'

Her nipples had peaked beneath his fingers and the sensations she was coming to know well were starting to wash through her. Desire, like a lovely tide, flowed from her breasts to the secret, sensitive core of her and was so strong she gasped his name in a plea, to tell him it was more than she could bear. But he was as ready as she was. Their love-making was swift, yet utterly splendid, and left her shuddering in his arms, clinging to him and he to her.

'Was that rushed or what?' he murmured at last, and buried his face in the curve of her shoulder.

'Whatever, it was wonderful.' She threaded her fingers through his hair. 'Could there be something to be said for an afternoon nap?'

'In so much as I woke up with this on my mind, yes,' he agreed ruefully. 'And I'll tell you something else.' He lifted his head and looked laughingly into her eyes. 'If you thought I was smug before, it's nothing to how I feel now.'

'I see,' she replied gravely. 'How do you think I feel?'

'Uh...wonderful?'

'You are *incredibly* smug, Damien Moore,' she told him severely, then relented. 'Unfortunately I can't tell you that you're wrong.'

'Then perhaps I can tell you, Lee, that thanks to you I feel so wonderful I'm about to leap up and drag you off for a swim.'

'It's dark,' she protested.

'There's a light on the spit and the tide's still high, so we won't have to go far out, and these are very placid waters.'

'You're right. OK.' She jumped off the bed and pulled her bikini on. 'Race you!'

The water was wonderful, and they frolicked for about half an hour.

'This is gorgeous,' Lee enthused as she surfaced and Damien pulled her into his arms.

'You're gorgeous,' he told her.

She laughed down at him as water streamed off her. 'Actually, I meant you too, and the water.' She put her hands on his shoulders and her legs around his waist. 'I just wish I didn't have to go home tomorrow.' She stopped and looked surprised.

He kissed her. 'So do I.'

Her eyes widened, but he said no more.

After they'd showered together he left her to get dressed at her leisure and said he'd meet her on the deck for dinner in half an hour. He didn't say why.

Lee took her time. She'd found a French boutique in Vila and updated her wardrobe in a small way. And in the duty-free shops at Brisbane airport she'd treated herself to some luxury cosmetics. They made her feel luxurious now, as she smoothed delicately perfumed moisturiser all over her body and made up her face lightly. Then she pulled one of the two dresses she'd bought over her head. It was long, light and silky, with a halter top, in a delicate shade of topaz with tiny jade sprigs.

Coincidentally, it was not a dress you wore a bra with, she thought as she brushed her hair vigorously and watched it settle in a shining auburn cloud to her shoulders. Then again, coincidentally, she mused as she laid her brush down, she'd had the deepest misgivings about coming to Vanuatu with Damien. But here she was, loving every minute of it—and more in love with him than ever.

She studied her reflection in the mirror. Her tan had deepened to pale gold; her eyes were strikingly green. She looked well, better than she'd ever looked in her life, she thought. But how long would she be able to keep at bay the misgivings that lay just below the surface of her mind? Precisely, where would they go from here?

She swallowed, then forced herself to relax. She sprayed some French perfume on, and went to meet Damien.

Tables were set out on the deck over the water, and braziers flamed and smoked gently along the perimeter. Two waitresses in pretty smocks were moving amongst the diners— Vanuatan women had a traditional dress, V-necked with puff sleeves, generally in floral cotton, loose and tiered, and often trimmed with ribbon streamers, and the Erakor ladies wore yellow and pink floral, trimmed with yellow.

The tables were lit with little paraffin lamps and decked with hibiscus blooms. If you were seated beside the rail of the deck you could see the fish swimming below, and the resident eel that made nightly forays amongst the clouds of little fish. Palm trees and causurinas fringed the deck and cast twisted shadows on it.

Damien was nowhere to be seen. Lee hesitated and was about to turn towards the main dining room, a traditional, palm-thatched structure with open sides and cyclone shutters propped up on bamboo poles, when a hand slipped into hers.

'Going my way, Mrs Moore?'

She looked up into Damien's dark eyes. 'I—think so.'

He studied her comprehensively for a long moment, taking in the cool, simple but chic dress, the sheen of her skin and lips, the wonderful hair—and the suddenly uncertain look in her eyes. 'What's wrong?'

She shook her head. 'Nothing. I couldn't see you, that's all.'

His fingers tightened on hers for a moment. Then he said lightly, 'We have our same table. I hope you're hungry.' And he led her towards it.

The head waiter immediately descended on them with the wine list and the menu board. Lee chose the reef and beef kebabs—the beef on Vanuatu was the tenderest, tastiest beef she'd had for years, and the reef component was barbecued prawns, which she adored.

Damien ordered the same, but it wasn't until their bottle of wine was opened and tasted that he said, 'It's all arranged.'

She looked at him enquiringly over the rim of her wine glass.

'Another favourite spot of mine is the Tamanu Beach Club. I've changed our flights and booked us in there for two

nights. It's different from Erakor, on an unprotected surf
beach, but in its own way just as nice.'

She gazed at him, surprised into speechlessness.

'You don't approve?' There was just a hint of his former
arrogance in his voice, and his eyes were unreadable.

She looked away, down at the fish in the lit, clear pale
aqua water below the deck, and her voice was husky as she
spoke. 'I'm sure I would approve, but why didn't you ask
me first?'

'What's to ask?' he countered. 'You seem to have fallen
in love with Vanuatu.'

She gestured and sipped some more wine. 'I have. My
grandparents are expecting me back tomorrow, though.'

'No, they're not. I've just spoken to them. I have their
permission to keep you away for a week.' He looked quizzical. 'It won't be that long, but, trust me, you'll love
Tamanu.'

Several emotions gathered within Lee. The most disturbing
was the urge to tell him that *that* was the problem—she had
no doubt she'd love the place, if he liked it so much, but
how much further would it enhance the enchantment of being
with him and how much harder would it make it when the
time came to go their separate ways?

'Lee,' he said abruptly, 'tell me what's going on behind
those wonderful eyes. Is it just pique because I didn't consult
you? I thought it would be a pleasant surprise.'

It came to her then, out of the blue, that she'd made her
own bed—in a more than apt manner of speaking. She'd
offered herself to Damien Moore because she hadn't been
able to resist him. But that was her problem, not his, and it
was her responsibility to handle whatever came in the future,
not his. Not that this knowledge would make it any easier,
she knew, but it brought her a curious sense of peace...

Accordingly, she wrinkled her nose playfully at him and
said, 'I guess we each have our crosses to bear. You can be
insufferably *right* about things at times. I can be—well, not

keen on having all decisions taken out of my hands. However, I have now abandoned "pique", and look forward to the…joys of Tamanu tomorrow.'

It had come out well, she thought as she stopped speaking. Just a slight hesitation over the word 'joys', but otherwise not bad.

His expression didn't change for a long moment, though, and she was beginning to revise her judgement of her own insouciance and powers of masking her true feelings—then his lips twisted and he started to laugh.

She breathed a hidden sigh of relief, and they enjoyed their dinner companionably.

'You know, I should have realised it before,' Lee said, 'but this is where James Michener based *Tales of the South Pacific,* one of my all-time favourite musicals. Not on this island, Erakor, but Santo. In the days when Vanuatu was known as the New Hebrides, during the Second World War, when the Americans had a huge base up there.'

'You've been doing your homework,' Damien replied. 'Actually, that's another place I'd like to show you— Bokissa, just off Santo. And, yes, I have seen Ambae Island, which Michener thought was the most beautiful island in the South Pacific and the island he based Bali Hi on. Legend has it that all the beautiful young women were sent to Ambae during the war to keep them away from the GIs. You like musicals?' he asked.

Lee looked a bit embarrassed. 'I'd hate to tell you how many times I've watched *The Sound of Music.*'

He grinned. 'Come to think of it, I've heard you whistling, humming and singing while you work—and yodelling when you're particularly happy about something.'

'"The Lonely Goatherd",' Lee acknowledged ruefully. 'I wish you hadn't brought that up. Once I start, it gets on my brain.'

He looked alarmed. 'So I shouldn't be too surprised if, in moments of high passion, a bit of yodelling emerges?'

Lee bit her lip, then started to smile. 'If you can make me yodel in bed, Damien, I won't know whether to die of shame or award you a medal! And I don't think— What I mean to say is, your heights are high enough as it is.' She stopped and could have shot herself as the colour rushed into her cheeks beneath the extremely speculative dark gaze beaming her way.

'Don't take that... That wasn't a challenge,' she said disjointedly. 'And don't forget that a lot of people hate yodelling, even if it's Julie Andrews, so it could spoil things—I can't believe I'm having this conversation with you!' She put her napkin on the table and pushed her plate away.

'I doubt if we could spoil things between us, Lee,' he said slowly, all the amusement suddenly leached from his expression.

She was still smarting, however, and she looked at him broodingly. 'Right now I feel like an act out of a sideshow.'

'Come with me and I'll prove to you you're not.'

'Again?'

'I'm afraid so. We'll take the rest of the wine with us.' He stood up.

Lee breathed uncertainly. She didn't know how to handle this, she thought confusedly. She had sensed a change in him at last—a change she didn't understand. And as he stood straight, tall and divine but unsmiling, in his khaki trousers and a black T-shirt, she was suddenly afraid that she didn't understand him at all.

But she followed him down the path to their bungalow and stood on the veranda while he poured the wine.

He handed her her glass.

She looked at the golden liquid, then raised her eyes to him abruptly. 'What happened?'

'Nothing.' He looked across the dark water to the lights twinkling on the mainland. 'Nothing. But maybe we should save ourselves for Tamanu.'

Her fingers tightened around the glass. She understood his mood even less.

'Maybe,' he said softly then, 'we should listen to the BBC World Service, which is all I can coax out of the radio, and talk.'

There was a comfortable cane couch on the veranda and she sank down onto it while he fiddled with the radio inside. All he could get was a learned discussion of Afghanistan and the Taliban, so he switched it off and came to join her on the couch, where he put his arm around her and she laid her head on his shoulder.

'Shoes, ships and ceiling wax, then?' Lee said. 'Is that what we need to talk about?'

He pulled her closer and kissed the top of her head. 'No. In the normal course of events this is when I would be asking you to marry me, Lee, but since that has already happened— What's wrong?' he asked as she moved restlessly.

CHAPTER EIGHT

'I'D PREFER cabbages and kings, that's all, Damien,' she said eventually, and forced herself to go on. 'This is all so romantic, and I have no doubt Tamanu will be also, but I don't think it's conducive to good decision-making.'

'You don't know what I'm about to propose.'

'No,' she agreed. 'But it would be fair to say that although you haven't made me yodel in bed yet, you have…kind of…got me all at sixes and sevens at the moment. In the nicest possible way,' she added. 'So don't feel I'm being critical—'

'Lee, shut up for a moment, will you?' he ordered.

'My lips are sealed,' she murmured, then laughed and tilted her face to brush her lips against his. 'By the way, I applaud your decision to practise some restraint tonight—'

He stopped her from uttering anything further by trapping her chin in his hand and kissing her thoroughly. So thoroughly, and pleasurably, that the idea of restraint began to be unthinkable, and she was, for once, speechless as she lay trembling against him, licking her bruised lips.

Then she heard him sigh. 'Perhaps you're right. Have I made you nervous, though?'

She blinked at him.

He shrugged wryly. 'You do tend to babble when you're nervous, I've learnt.'

It was her turn to sigh. 'I know,' she said sadly. 'It's always a sure sign that I don't know if I'm on my head or my heels.'

He laughed briefly, then held her close with unmistakable affection and tenderness. But love? she wondered. Like the real, everlasting love that she knew she would always feel

142

for him. The knowledge that no one could ever be so important to her. That magic attraction and depth of feeling for someone...

His mobile phone rang.

He swore, then moved her away from him, kissed her swiftly, and went inside to answer it. After a few minutes of terse conversation he came back to tell her, with a lurking smile in his eyes, that fate had intervened.

'You have to go somewhere?' she hazarded.

'Back into town for a couple of hours, but this will be the last time,' he promised.

She smiled. 'That's OK. I'll be here.'

She was, but by the time he got back she was fast asleep.

She'd left a lamp on and he stood beside the bed for a long moment, watching her sleep peacefully with one hand tucked beneath her cheek and her lovely hair spread across the pillow.

Nor did she stir as he sat down on the bed and took off his shoes.

It crossed his mind to wake her and take her, but then all sorts of strange ideas had been crossing his mind lately in relation to Lee Westwood, he reflected rather grimly. Ideas that made him wonder if this sometimes exasperating girl had got into his blood.

There was, for example, the way she'd handled the time he'd had to spend apart from her over the last few days. She hadn't appeared to mind being left to her own devices at all. Instead, she'd endeared herself to the staff and she'd thoroughly enjoyed Erakor.

And there was the kind of lover she was. A delight to put it plainly, he thought as he watched her sleep. Silken, sensitive, delicious, generous, but sometimes supremely vulnerable to the pleasure he inflicted on her—and that aroused an instinct that was new to him. Something that was protective.

something that didn't like the idea of that vulnerability falling into another man's hands and being exploited...

He chewed his lip and she stirred, but only to rearrange her gorgeous legs, say something inaudible then fall back into serene sleep.

He got up, pulled his clothes off, and slid in beside her. Even in sleep she melted against him, as if it was the most natural thing in the world.

Sleep did not come easily to him, however, as he held her slim body and breathed in her perfume. In fact he started to feel irritated.

She obviously didn't want to talk about the future, yet she could lie in his arms like this, with complete trust and serenity. She *had* been nervous when he'd brought the subject up, he reminded himself.

But the fact of the matter was, it now didn't seem like a bad idea to stay married to Lee Westwood—yet he had no idea what her thinking on the subject was. Strike that, he thought grimly, because he very much suspected she'd have all sorts of objections.

So... Well, there was always Tamanu, he told himself, and buried his face in her hair. There was always Tamanu...

'What do you think?' Damien Moore asked his wife-by-dissent the next morning.

Lee drew a deep breath. 'As if I can see for ever on a day like today. All the way to New Zealand!'

She was standing on the veranda of their bungalow at the Tamanu Beach Club, looking out to sea.

The beach was pale gold and the breaking surf was dazzlingly white against the different blues of the ocean—indigo towards the horizon, turquoise towards the beach. The air was salty and filled with the murmur of the waves. The pale blue sky was huge. The sand was fringed with pandanus palms—not lush and leafy as she'd seen on Erakor, but spindly and misshapen like a Chinese painting—possibly from the power of the onshore winds—although still bearing at the heart of each cluster of leaves a fruit like a giant pineapple.

The feeling of space and peace was incredible—and then there was the bungalow. She turned to look inside again.

It was built of white coral, with three French doors opening on to the veranda and wooden shutters at the windows; the floor was white-tiled. The double bed beneath a blue Aztec spread had a mosquito net draped from the ceiling, and there was a couch and chairs covered in the same Aztec print. Grouped on the coffee table, on the bed and studded along a lovely piece of driftwood were frilled red hibiscus blooms, their long stamens dusted with yellow tendrils. There was a garden bathroom, at the rear. It was quite private and quite delightful.

'A wonderful place to spend a honeymoon,' she said unthinkingly.

He looked down at her enigmatically, but said, 'Should we have a swim before lunch?'

'Why not?' she answered, but heard the uncertainty in her voice. Uncertainty because she had the distinct feeling she might have been brought to Tamanu for just that reason—a honeymoon...

He broke into her thoughts. 'We'll go to Fred's Hole. This beach is better at high tide. So bring your hat and don't forget your reef shoes!'

Lee stood to attention and saluted.

He laughed and kissed her. 'No cheek, either, Mrs Moore. The beach is littered with coral—pretty, but deadly underfoot.'

The beach *was* littered with coral—bleached white by the sun—and some marvellous shells as they walked south. The heat was tangible and she was glad of her hat and the T-shirt she'd put on to protect her from the sun's rays. Some rocky outcrops jutted into the water, and between two of them they found the cove called Fred's Hole. The water was clear and placid, because the mouth of the cove was protected by a reef, the bottom was sandy and it looked incredibly inviting.

Lee shed her shirt and hat and ran in, with Damien hot on her heels.

'Oh, what bliss!' she called, and dived beneath the surface.

They swam for about half an hour, then walked back to lunch, and things were so friendly, peaceful, and sometimes playful between them so that her concerns about being on a honeymoon receded. Mind you, she thought, it was hard to have any concerns in a place like this. The dining area was beneath a canopy, open on three sides, and the beach was right there in front of them.

She ordered a Tempura seafood and vegetable dish and it was superb. They shared a bottle of wine.

'This is pure decadence,' she told him. 'All I'll be good for is a sleep now!'

He raised his glass to her. 'I've got a better idea. There's a golf course close by.'

Lee groaned. 'You wouldn't!'

'I would. Come with me. The walk will do you good. I might even be able to instruct you in the finer points of the game. Then we could have another swim. I didn't think you were the kind of person who napped, incidentally.'

'I'm not.' She grimaced. 'But then I don't usually indulge in fine food and wine in the middle of the day—what time did you get back last night, by the way?'

'Shortly after ten o'clock. You were fast asleep.'

'I must have been.' She looked comical. 'Did...? Was...? No.' She looked away suddenly.

'Was that all right with me?' he queried softly. 'Yes and no. But we seemed to have agreed upon restraint so I did my best not to wake you.'

She ran her fingers through her hair and gathered it back.

'Tonight could be a different story, however,' he said barely audibly, and raised an eyebrow at her. 'Unless you have other ideas?'

Lee lowered her arms and his gaze rested squarely on her breasts. He noted how the movement altered the lie of her blouse—worn without a bra for once.

She trembled inwardly. 'Such as?'

'Such as telling the golf course to get lost.'

'I...no, I don't think that would be a very good idea. I think it will be cooler tonight, for one thing.'

His lips twisted. 'Cooler in one sense, certainly. I thought you always wore a bra, Lee?'

She looked down and could see the outline of her nipples against the fine white cotton. 'I...will from now on.'

'I wish you wouldn't.' He sat back. 'That wasn't a criticism.'

Lee looked around, but no one was looking their way or appeared to be tuned into their conversation. And perhaps something about the sheer beauty of Tamanu was liberating. She didn't know, but she picked up her wine glass, swallowed the last of the chilled contents and said huskily, 'All the same, there should still be a lovely moon tonight.'

He raised one eyebrow thoughtfully. 'That sounds—promising.'

She smiled a secret little smile and told him she would like a cup of coffee, a bit of time to digest her lunch—and then she would be ready for golf.

The other new dress Lee had purchased in Vila was white, short, sleeveless, with a square neck and buttoned down the front. She'd tucked a hibiscus in her hair for dinner, but although feeling she looked the part—chic but casual and cast-away, in tune with Tamanu—she hadn't eaten a lot.

She had no illusions as to why her appetite appeared to have deserted her.

The golf had been fun, the swim afterwards heavenly, and all through it they'd been friendly and playful with each other. They'd barely got back from the beach when they'd been invited to have pre-dinner drinks with the manager of the club and his wife, and that had been enjoyable too. All the same there had been a spiralling core of tension within her. And what had generated it was the way Damien's dark eyes had rested on her from time to time.

He had barely touched her all afternoon, had said nothing particularly intimate, but at the same time he had deliberately increased the sensual tension between them in a way that had been almost tangible—to Lee, at least. And she'd got quieter and quieter beneath this mysterious onslaught, less and less sure of herself, with the odd notion that he had turned into a stranger before her eyes.

Now, as she stood on the cool white tiles of their bungalow, watching the moon rise through the French doors, she found she couldn't speak at all—so much for her cool, come-hither approach at lunch.

Damien had not bothered with lights when they'd come in, but had lit one candle on the bedside table, and in its flickering glow he stood before her—tall, dark and somehow dangerous.

'The time has come, my lady,' he said very quietly.

She swallowed, and didn't realise that she looked like a wide-eyed, startled fawn about to bolt...

'May I?' He touched the top button of her dress.

'I...' she temporised—to gain time? she wondered. Then she knew there was no escaping—she didn't even know what she was afraid of, other than the electric charge that was between them and the sheer power of it. 'Yes...' she whispered.

He freed each button carefully and the dress slid to the floor, revealing her figure in a white lacy bra and high-cut bikini briefs.

An absent smile twisted his lips and he ran his fingers beneath the lace that covered the tops of her breasts. 'Old habits die hard.'

She licked her lips. 'Lunch taught me a lesson, I guess.'

He undid the bra and slid it off, then stopped touching her. 'Why are you looking like this, Lee?'

'Like...?'

'Petrified,' he said quietly.

She breathed raggedly but couldn't answer.

'I thought, if nothing else, you trusted me.'

'I do. I...it's strange.' She tried to articulate her feelings. 'I'm filled with fear...and longing at the same time. I don't know why.' Or did she? she wondered.

'Perhaps I can help,' he said after an age. He'd been staring intently into her confused green eyes with a frown in his own, but now he looked briefly down her body, the flickering candlelight casting tantalising shadows on the slim, golden length of her, and left her for a moment to gather her short robe from a hook in the bathroom.

Surprise lit her eyes as he helped her into it and belted the soft green cotton at her waist. Then he took her hand and led her to the bed, already turned down for the night. She hesitated, then lay down, and he left her again—but only to pull his shirt and trousers off and pull on a pair of pyjama bottoms. Then he climbed in beside her and took her loosely in his arms.

'You know where I went wrong?' he said softly. 'I didn't like to think you could resist me at lunch. I don't mind preaching restraint, but I'm not at all keen on the thought that you can actually practise it. Correspondingly...' He paused. 'I've spent the rest of the damn day trying to punish you for your serenity and restraint without even realising it— realising I was frightening the life out of you by building this up into a monumental encounter of some kind, with a stranger.'

Lee trembled in his arms, amazed at his honesty and understanding. But was that all of it? she wondered.

'So,' he said, and stroked her hair rhythmically, 'will you let me make amends for being a monumental fool?'

'Yes, please,' she whispered, and felt herself relaxing for

the first time for hours. 'But I feel like a bit of an idiot. It's not as if I'm a scared virgin.'

'More of a virgin than you suspect,' he said, then added immediately, 'No, don't ask me to explain—and it has nothing to do with you being a less than delightful lover, should your mind make the kind of quantum leap it has a habit of doing.'

Lee was silent for a moment, then she laughed quietly. She lay in his arms and felt warmed and cherished as he caressed her very gently. Then she sat up and pulled her robe off.

'If I was nervous before, I'm something quite different now,' she murmured, and she bent to touch her lips to his and brush her breasts against the wall of his chest.

'Sure?'

'Oh, yes. See for yourself.'

He did more. He stripped her panties off and explored the secret, most sensitive depths of her. Then he pulled the pillows up behind him and eased her on top of him in a sitting position.

She gasped as he entered her, tightening her fingers in the dark springy hair of his chest as he alternately played with her nipples and cupped her bottom. 'That's...lovely,' she said huskily.

'You're lovely,' he responded. 'It would be hard to know what my preferences are in regard to you, Lee. Breasts, bottom, legs—they're all gorgeous, my lady—sorry, strike that!'

'No, don't strike it. I like it now,' she breathed. 'And I like this...too much,' she added as he moved. 'May I come down before...?'

'Be my guest,' he murmured, and drew her into his arms. 'It's not exactly easy for me either...well, see what I mean?'

'Yes,' she gasped as they moved as one, and then all she could do was bury her face in his shoulder as they were carried away on a higher tide than even Damien had brought to her before.

*   *   *

'I didn't...did I?' she asked cautiously, some time later.

He tightened his arms about her spent body and kissed her. 'Yodel? No.' He sounded amused. 'Did you feel like it?'

She was silent for a moment. 'No,' she said at last. 'Nothing is good enough to...salute that.' She shuddered in his arms just at the memory of it. 'Thank you.'

'You have a strange notion of where thanks are due, Lee.'

She lifted her head and regarded him gravely. 'There may be a lot of things you can dictate, Damien, but where I place my thanks is not one of them.'

'Lee—'

'Don't argue,' she recommended. 'However...' she turned away from him, although stayed within reach '...if you would like to hold me while we fall asleep, that would be acceptable.'

He sat up and bent over her. 'Yes, ma'am. On the condition that I'm allowed to kiss you goodnight first.'

Lee sighed theatrically. 'That's like always having to have the last word!'

'On the contrary. I will feel...unfinished otherwise.'

She turned slowly. 'I think you're teasing me.'

He trapped her between his arms. 'Perish the thought.'

She looked into his dark, wicked eyes, and was surprised when they suddenly sobered. 'What now?' she asked hesitantly.

He took his time.

The disarray of her hair was gorgeous against the pillow, the green of her eyes soft in the candlelight. He turned his head and blew the candle out, and after a while their eyes adjusted to the silvery moonlight flooding into the room.

'I just wanted to say—thank *you*, my lovely moon-maiden.' He kissed her and she clung to him, exceptionally moved.

The flight home was smooth and they came into Brisbane over the South Passage Bar—Damien pointed out Day's Gutter on Moreton Island.

During their second day and night at Tamanu and on the flight they'd discussed nothing beyond the present. But their closeness had been special. It was only now, as the aircraft descended over Moreton Bay, that Lee had to wonder what the future held.

'It's Friday,' Damien said as the wheels touched down. They were holding hands.

'About nine o'clock in the morning?'

He agreed with a smile twisting his lips. 'I have to go into the office for a few hours. What would you like to do?'

'I should think about getting home somehow—'

'No.' His fingers tightened over hers. 'We'll go down together tomorrow. Why don't you relax in the apartment? I'm going there first anyway.'

'All right,' she said, after a moment's thought that had produced a blank mind.

He raised her hand and kissed her knuckles. 'Trust me, Lee,' he said quietly.

But there was a surprise waiting for them at the apartment.

Damien unlocked the door and frowned as the aroma of freshly made coffee assailed their nostrils. 'Who…?' He stopped, then ushered Lee over the doorstep. 'It's got to be Melinda, my sister. I told you about her.'

'Damien…' Lee hesitated, then it was too late.

A tall, dark woman came swiftly into the foyer. She was as good-looking in her own way as her brother, and quite a lot like him—that same air of assurance. She was beautifully dressed in a turquoise linen dress that shouted couturier, exquisitely groomed, and she moved on a wave of French perfume.

'Damien!' she said delightedly, then stopped as if shot as her gaze fell on Lee. 'Is this…? Is this…?'

'This is Lee, Mel—my wife,' Damien said simply.

'Oh, dear! I mean...' Melinda swallowed visibly. 'I'm so pleased to meet you, Lee. Mother told me all about you...but...you're the last person I expected—I mean...' She stopped helplessly.

Damien eyed her sardonically for a moment. Then he drawled, 'Things have changed since I last discussed them with our august parent, Mel. Lee and I have just come back from our...honeymoon.'

Melinda looked truly appalled. Then she said in a frantic undertone, 'But I've got Julia here!'

Damien swore. 'What the bloody hell for?'

'I...I...she rang me and asked if she could come up for a chat. I'm only down for a couple of days and I've got wall-to-wall meetings—this is the only free time I had.'

Damien swore again, and turned to Lee. 'This could call for SWAT mode, my dear. Don't look like that,' he added softly. 'You didn't really think I was going to let you go, did you?'

'But...but...' Lee stammered.

'Just be yourself,' he recommended.

'But who is she?' Lee asked desperately.

'Don't you remember? She's the person my mother so helpfully filled you in about.'

It was hard to know who was more discomfited at first.

Julia Blake-Whitney was another tall, elegant woman, although blonde, with that innate air of assurance, exquisite grooming and the kind of clothes that wouldn't look out of place on a Chanel catwalk.

And although her poise deserted her upon being introduced to Lee, it was only briefly.

Melinda was definitely discomfited as she fussed about, insisting on making more coffee. And Lee was tongue-tied for the first few minutes as she watched Julia regain her poise. Only Damien exhibited no signs that this meeting was in any way awkward.

He strode forward to greet Julia with his hand outstretched and a faint smile playing on his lips. 'Julia, this is Lee,' he said. 'I guess Melinda has filled you in—or perhaps you saw the write-up of Ella's famous *Gilligan's Island* party?'

Julia Blake-Whitney dazedly shook his hand and agreed disjointedly that she had. She then looked directly at Lee, taking in her jeans and pink blouse, her complete lack of make-up and loose hair. She blinked twice.

Lee barely managed to refrain from looking down at her clothes herself. At least her jeans were new, and her pink blouse quite acceptable, and instead of her inevitable boots she wore a pair of polished leather moccasins. But she felt light years away from these two polished, perfumed, obviously sophisticated women, and thoroughly self-conscious for a while.

It was Damien who held the fort. He sprawled out in an armchair, accepted a cup of coffee from his sister and told them all about Vanuatu.

Julia recovered first. She had been to Vanuatu twice and was able to swap experiences, which she did so animatedly, giving Lee a glimpse of the vital personality to match her golden good looks and beautiful, expressive grey eyes. In fact the thought slid across Lee's mind that Julia Blake-Whitney was a perfect match for Damien Moore...

Then Julia said smoothly, although with a distinct hint of irony, 'I'm sure it's a great place for a honeymoon, however belated.'

Talk about being caught on the horns of a dilemma, was Lee's next thought. I haven't agreed to anything yet—I don't even know what Damien has in mind—I'm still reeling from being told he has no intention of letting me go...and now this ex-lover of his is testing me out!

'It was lovely,' she heard herself say. She paused and thought of Erakor and Tamanu, and drew strength from her memories. She smiled suddenly. 'Even although it was a belated honeymoon, I'll never forget it.'

True enough, she thought in the sudden little silence her words produced, and take that, Julia Blake-Whitney, even although you may not deserve it!

Melinda sprang into the breach. She looked at her watch and groaned. 'Sorry, but I have to fly!' She stood up.

Julia did the same. 'I've got an appointment as well, so I really should make a move. Well, Damien.' She turned to him. 'All best wishes! And of course to you too, Lee.'

Damien rose. 'I'll see you out, Julia. Hang on a moment, Melinda.'

Melinda sank back and watched Damien and Julia walk out. Then she turned her dark eyes to Lee and said helplessly, 'Mum...she told me it was a marriage of convenience. She also told me to stay out of it. Apparently Damien warned her off pretty brutally. Then Julia rang me on my mobile last night. She thought I was in Cairns, but I was here collecting my things, and she asked if she could just come and have a chat—we went to school together. I feel terrible! But—'

'You weren't to know,' Damien supplied dryly, coming back into the lounge.

Some spirit sparked in Melinda's dark eyes. 'No, I was not, Damien! We all felt you and Julia would get back—' She stopped and bit her lip, then looked rebellious again. 'If you didn't keep us in this fog of ignorance, it mightn't have happened.' She turned to Lee, 'Lee, forgive me. But that is the truth of the matter. However, welcome to the family!'

Lee had risen, and Melinda walked over to her and hugged her awkwardly. Then she stood back and said with some humour, 'I may not know what's going on, I may have put my foot in my mouth several times—but I do mean that.'

Ten minutes later, Melinda had departed.

'She's nice,' Lee murmured as the door closed on Damien's sister.

He shrugged and looked irritable for a moment.

'It could have happened to anyone,' Lee offered.

His look changed to one of wryness. 'It could only happer to my sister or my mother. Did you mean what you said?'

Lee didn't pretend to misunderstand. 'About never forgetting Vanuatu? Yes. But—'

'Lee,' he forestalled her, 'I meant what *I* said.'

She turned away from him, but he put his hands on her shoulders and turned her back. 'I'm sorry if it came out dictatorially, I'm sorry we haven't discussed it before, but you were the one who didn't want to.'

She looked up into his dark eyes. 'Why did they think you and Julia would get back together?'

His fingers dug into her shoulders for a moment. 'I have no idea,' he said shortly, then set his teeth for a moment 'Julia and Melinda have been friends for years and years; suppose that's why Mel wanted it. And I told you what my mother's main aim in life for me is—to carry on the name.

'There must have been more to it than that,' Lee said qui etly. 'You must have been good together, you and Julia. I'm sure neither your mother nor your sister would want you to marry someone you didn't love.'

He started to say something, then paused and studied he intently. 'We were,' he said at last, 'to all intents and pur poses the ideal couple, Lee. She's a scratch golfer, her famil breeds horses on a famous stud, she's also a lawyer, and can't deny that we were together for two years. But ther was something missing that I couldn't put my finger on— something that always stopped me from asking her to marr me. I still don't know what it was but when she forced th issue, I backed out as decently as I could.'

'May I make a suggestion?' Lee asked very quietly.

'What do you mean?'

'That you tell me exactly what kind of a future you pro pose for us, Damien.'

'That we stay married,' he said impatiently. 'I thought tha much was obvious.'

'Yes,' she conceded. 'But how? You spending most o

your life up here and me spending most of mine at Plover Park?'

This time when he paused she thought it was to choose his words with care. She wasn't proved wrong. 'I think that would work extremely well for us. You love Plover Park and this way you could keep it.' His lips twisted. 'Although if you ever change your mind about how you would like to spend your life, there's more than enough room here.'

Lee swallowed and looked around. 'I could never sit here twiddling my thumbs.'

The look he shot her told her that she had just proved his point, but he shrugged. 'It doesn't necessarily have to be here. My mother has always said she'll move out of the house when I marry—it is mine, anyway.'

She hesitated. 'What if I choose Plover Park and we have children?'

'I can't think of a better place to bring up kids—Lee...' He drew her against him and kissed her hair. 'What is it you're trying to say?'

She trembled in his arms. 'I couldn't do it, Damien. I would feel like a long-distance wife. We're just too... Our worlds are too far apart for it ever to work.'

'Rubbish,' he said. 'We have the best reasons in the world to make a go of it. We're both the kind of people who don't like living in anyone's pocket—' He stopped abruptly as she freed herself.

She stood straight, slender and pale in front of him, her freckles standing out noticeably. 'If Julia had been happy not to live in your pocket, Damien, don't you think that might have removed whatever it was you couldn't put your finger on?'

'Which is, precisely?' he drawled, his eyes suddenly cool and his mouth hard.

'Precisely? That a marriage of convenience, ensuring order and heirs, is what you really want.'

CHAPTER NINE

'ARE you suggesting that I would like to have my cake and eat it, Lee? A wife to produce heirs and a mistress to enjoy myself with?'

If she was pale, then so was he now, and the tension in the air was electric. But it was a tension threaded with anger—his anger.

'N-not immediately, perhaps,' she said unevenly, and gestured a little helplessly.

'You don't think that kind of marriage went out with Regency times?' He raised his eyebrows and looked at her satirically.

She swallowed. 'I have it on good authority that it has its appeal—especially for men.'

'Who's authority?'

'I can't tell you that, and anyway—' she shook her head '—it's not that. I'm not basing my objections on...on that.'

'On what, then?' he grated lethally.

Why had she started this? Lee wondered despairingly. Had meeting Julia infected her with...what? More doubt than she already cherished? Or were her objections based solely on the type of marriage he was proposing, as well as the fact that he was using Plover Park as a lure? But what else would work for them?

'Talk to me, Lee,' he said dangerously. 'I know I took pains to reassure you at Tamanu, but if you can't come up with something better than you've so far produced I wouldn't be averse to persuading your body to speak for you—extremely pleasurably for both of us.' He raked her figure insolently with his dark gaze.

She gasped. 'You wouldn't!'

'Don't bet on it,' he warned. 'And let's not forget something else. Who seduced whom, initially?'

'That…that has nothing to do with this!' she stammered.

He laughed, softly and scornfully. 'No?'

Lee closed her eyes. 'Why do you think Julia wanted to speak to Melinda?' she asked.

'Lee, *that* has nothing to do with this. I finished with Julia before I ever married you. She doesn't enter into this equation at all.'

Lee flinched visibly and kept her lashes lowered. A mistake. Because that was when Damien abandoned his verbal assault and began a physical assault. Not that it felt like an assault, he was too clever for that…

He kissed the tears beading her lashes, then cupped her face and kissed her mouth. 'You know what you taste of?' he said softly. 'Tamanu—still a little salty from our last dawn swim this morning. Remember how you woke up?'

She remembered all too well. She'd opened her eyes to just a faint lightening of the sky, and the thought that they were leaving Vanuatu today had gripped her and filled her with apprehension. She'd turned to Damien urgently and buried herself in his arms. They'd made urgent love without a word being spoken, then, in all the glory of a deep-rose sunrise, they'd had their last swim.

Was it only this morning? she thought with surprise. It almost seemed part of another life.

'You made love to me as if your world was falling apart this morning, Lee,' he said very quietly. 'But it doesn't have to be that way.'

She looked into his eyes at last, hers mirroring her shock at what she'd unwittingly given away in the dawn hours.

'You…' she breathed, and couldn't go on.

'I'm honoured,' he said simply. 'And I promise you, you won't regret it.' He picked her up and carried her into the master bedroom.

She was too stunned to resist when he undressed her, then too aroused by what he did to her to take issue with anything.

What could you do, she wondered, with a man who played your body like the finest violin so that it sang for him; a man who took your breath away and made you feel like a living flame in his arms, not only pleasured almost out of your mind but desirous of pleasing him? What could you do with a man who said the kind of things he said to her?

Such as... 'Lee, do you know how many words that start with L describe you?'

'Uh...no...'

'Lithe, lissome, lovely, languorous, lambent, luscious—'

'Damien, they can't all,' she said with an effort. 'But there is one more I could add—*lost*! Or I will be very soon, if you keep doing that.'

'This?' he asked lazily. She was lying on her back, he was on his side, with his dark head propped on his elbow and the fingers of his free hand laying a devastating trail of sensation very slowly up and down her body. He circled her breast and touched her nipples, then continued downwards across her stomach to the auburn curls at the base of it. There they rested for a fleeting moment. She shivered with delicious anticipation, made a low husky sound in her throat, and moved luxuriously to open her legs.

At the same time she slid her fingertips down the strong column of his throat, played a little with the springy dark hair of his chest, then continued her featherlight exploration of the hard planes of his body.

'Lee—' He stopped what he was doing, and her hand stilled. 'You're entering dangerous territory.'

Her lips tilted into a faint smile. 'You know all those words that start with L? Well, the only one I can think of that describe you that starts with D is just that—dangerous. Or come to think of it, downright dangerous!' Her hand started to move again, very slowly.

'But you don't mind?'

'Perhaps I'm adventurous at heart. Perhaps I am more of a one-woman SWAT team than I knew...' She paused as her voice caught in her throat. 'Because I'm just dying for you to be as downright dangerous as you like.'

'That,' he said unevenly, 'should do it.' And he swept her into his arms to enter her powerfully.

She revelled in it, moulding her slim length and soft curves to him but freeing her arms so she could wrap them around him. He eased her onto her back and their rhythm became a symphony, and she gloried not only in his strength but the mingling of their limbs, skin on skin, the smell and the taste of him, and finally their crescendo that literally caused her to see stars behind her closed lids.

She was still uttering sobbing little breaths when he rolled away from her, but only to pull her on top of him and anchor her there firmly, with his arms around her waist.

She opened her eyes cautiously, then could only lay her cheek against his shoulder until her breathing steadied.

'So,' he said, and stroked her hair gently, 'all signed and sealed, Lee?'

A fluttering little sigh escaped her lips. She could no more fight him or think of any other decision to make at this moment than she could fly to the moon, she realised. She couldn't even raise the indignation she should probably feel at being forced to accept his will in the matter at a time like this. Which said something, she thought. That he had a very strong point. Not exactly a weapon that was going to help her...

'Lee?'

She raised her head at last and he tucked some damp tendrils of hair behind her ears. His eyes were very dark, and it pleased her to see that his forehead was beaded with sweat. All the same, the question in his eyes was inescapable, and it occurred to her that Damien Moore might be deliciously dangerous in bed, but he was also extremely dangerous in the matter of getting his own way.

As if you didn't know that, Lee, she chided herself, and cleared her throat to speak. What came out was a surprise to her, though. She said huskily, 'OK, José, I'll give it a go. That's all I can think of at the moment.'

He laughed, then sobered. 'Why don't I skip work and we go home?'

A curious feeling of warmth flooded Lee. 'Are you sure?'

'Well, I need to make a few calls, but I should be ready to leave in an hour or so. You could have a long soak in the tub, or you could wander around and decide if there's anything you'd like to change here.'

Lee's eyes widened.

He shrugged. 'It's your home too.'

'I don't think I'd be game to change a hair of its head, so to speak.'

A wicked grin tugged at his lips. 'Are you not my interior designer extraordinaire?'

Her hand flew to her lips. 'Byron Bay—I'd forgotten all about it!'

He rolled over with her and kissed her lightly. 'I like the sound of that.'

'But...what do you mean?'

His dark eyes were alive with amusement. 'I like the thought of being able to drive all else from your mind, Lee.'

She coloured faintly, but said with dignity, 'Vanuatu had something to do with it too.'

'Of course,' he replied gravely. '*Viva* Vanuatu! I was the guy who took you there, however. Surely that deserves some recognition?'

She pretended to consider.

'Lee,' he said dangerously, 'if you have any plans of leaving this bed in the near future—'

'Damien,' she broke in hastily, 'I think you've done enough damage for one day—OK, it was the fantastic combination of you and Vanuatu!'

'Damage?' There was a slight frown in his eyes now.

'Yes, damage,' she said softly. 'You've wrecked me twice today—very nicely, but wrecked all the same.'

He hesitated and searched her eyes, but they were clear though a little shy. Then he said gravely, 'OK, I'll accept equal billing with your favourite South Pacific Island on one condition.'

She raised an eyebrow.

'That we do this again in the near future.'

'I...don't see any problem with that, Mr Moore.'

He laughed, kissed her again, then got up, tucked her in modestly and strode through to the bathroom.

Lee stayed where she was while he showered, and treated herself to the pleasure of watching him dress.

He pulled on clean jeans, then sat down on the side of the bed to put on his socks. Lee lay as still as a mouse with her arms beside her above the sheet—in awe, she realised, because he was so beautifully made.

Not that it came as any surprise to her. Vanuatu had really revealed his physique, as well as tanned it, but it still always came as a joy to her. The width of his shoulders, his compact hips and taut diaphragm, the line of dark hair disappearing into his jeans as he stood up and reached for the shirt.

And as her nerve-ends started to tingle their gazes caught and held. She was not to know there was something helpless in her expression. Helplessly star-struck...

Nor did she understand why he looked briefly grim, then sat down beside her again and spoke quietly and gently. 'I know this may typify all the things I'm bad at—running roughshod over people, for example.' He looked rueful. 'But trust me, Lee. I won't let you down.'

He picked up her hand and kissed her knuckles. 'Have a rest, my lady,' he added. 'We've got all day to get home.'

She did rest for a while, bodily, but mentally she was trying to grapple with the enormity of the decision she'd taken. And a little refrain kept running through her musings—his words *Trust me, Lee*. Was that *Trust me not to hurt you, Lee?* And did he know, though, that the very fact he hadn't said *I love you* was a hurt of its own, even though she seemed to be hopelessly bound to him?

And what proportion of his feelings for her, whatever they were, included a sense of responsibility? Responsibility for the fact she had fallen in love with him?

She pulled his pillow into her arms and breathed deeply. He had also said *You didn't really think I'd let you go, Lee*. Maybe that was what she should concentrate on. Maybe she should abrogate all her concerns and simply go with the flow. Because there was one thing that was in no doubt at all. She loved Damien Moore whatever he felt for her.

She did take a long soak in the tub, then dressed again in her jeans and pink blouse and went to find her husband.

He was on the phone, so she wandered into the kitchen and made them some coffee. He was still on the phone by the time she'd finished hers, so she took his advice and wandered around the apartment. Not that she was looking at it with a decorator's eye—or even a wife's eye, she thought with a grimace. Not yet. Would she ever? she wondered, as she stood in the doorway of the formal dining room.

The table had a vast glass top set on three intricately carved marble pedestals. The chairs were wrought-iron and powder-coated, to match the beige marble of the pedestals, with amber velvet seats. And a marvellous marble elephant, gorgeously caparisoned with jewel-bright colours, scarlet, jade, sapphire and amber, stood in the centre of the table. The walls of the dining room were hung with beige slub silk and the windows looked over the river to the tall glass towers on the opposite bank.

Lee suddenly found her mind drifting and adjusting the scenario in her imagination... She pictured the room at night, lit by candles, with the city lights across the river twinkling against a midnight-blue sky. She pictured the table set with gold and crystal, perhaps ecru linen placemats and napkins. She pictured herself and Damien welcoming guests into the dining room, she directing them to their places.

What would she be wearing? Something long that shimmered as she moved, with her hair drawn back and a comb or a flower securing it. She pictured herself as poised and relaxed, the perfect foil for her tall, dark husband who would be devastatingly attractive in...

Musical chimes interrupted her thoughts, and she came back to earth to hear Damien calling out, asking her to answer the door with a tinge of impatience in his voice.

It was Ella Patroni, and it was hard to say who was the more surprised of the two of them. Although Ella recovered quickly.

'Lee,' she said delightedly. 'So you've moved in at last! That's wonderful. Now I might be able to talk to someone, instead of leaving messages on Damien's machine that he never answers!'

'I...well...come in,' Lee invited. 'It's good to see you too,' she said, and realised she meant it as she led Ella into the lounge.

Damien came through from the study at the sound of their voices and smacked the palm of his hand to his head as he saw Ella. 'I'm sorry—I'm sorry, I'm *sorry*, Ella!'

'So you should be,' Ella remonstrated. 'You never answer my messages!'

'I just haven't had the time. We've been away, and I spent a lot of time down on the farm before that,' he explained.

'Then you're forgiven,' Ella said promptly, as the phone in Damien's study rang again and he looked over his shoulder. 'So, shoo back to work,' she instructed him, 'and I will consult with Lee.'

'You're a peach,' he said with a lurking grin. 'I'm sure Lee will look after you.'

*   *   *

Lee made fresh coffee and took Ella into the den.

'I'm sorry there's nothing to eat—not that I can find anyway. I don't really know my way around Damien's kitchen yet.'

'All to the good,' Ella said as she lowered her bulk into an armchair. 'I'm on a diet. So. You obviously haven't stayed here often?'

'Once.' Lee grimaced. 'After your party. We only got back from Vanuatu this morning.'

Ella sipped her coffee, then put it down with a frown. 'I'm renowned for my plain speaking, Lee,' she warned. 'Nothing I do seems to prevent me from putting my foot in my mouth at times. If we're going to be friends, I thought I should warn you.'

A half-smile played over Lee's lips. 'Concerning Damien and I,' she said quietly, 'it's all too easy to put your foot in your mouth. The same thing happened with his sister this morning.'

Ella blinked several times. 'Then,' she said slowly, 'you don't mind if I tell you that the mystery of your marriage is driving us all crazy?'

Lee looked away briefly and resisted the temptation to tell Ella that she suffered the same syndrome at times—including about an hour ago.

'But whatever took him away from Julia and brought him to you, it's working now?' Ella said softly.

Lee swallowed and saw again in her mind's eye the dining room as she had imagined it. But this time, in a dress that glittered as she moved, she pictured Julia Blake-Whitney partnering Damien...

'I...' She paused.

'I never thought she was the right one for him,' Ella said flatly.

It was Lee's turn to blink. 'You didn't?'

'No. Oh...' Ella waved a careless hand. 'She was gorgeous, gifted and all the rest, but lacking an essential ingredient Damien needs—little though he may realise it.'

'What's that?' Lee asked, her eyes huge.

'*Je ne sais quoi.* That certain something that's so hard to put into words.' Ella shrugged. 'I may not quite be able to put my finger on it, but I thought it was missing between them. And I don't know why...' she gazed at Lee '...but maybe, just maybe, you provide it, Lee.'

'I wish I knew what it might be, because to be honest this started out as a marriage of convenience, and I think—although...some things have changed—' Lee looked down at her hands and wondered why she was confiding in a virtual stranger. 'I think it still is.'

Ella surged up and came over to sit next to Lee on the settee. She put her arm around her. 'I gather your feelings for him aren't "convenient" in the slightest?'

'You gather right,' Lee said a little dryly.

'Then hang in there, kid,' Ella advised, and hugged her. 'Because I think you're special.'

'That's so kind—'

'Rubbish, it's true!' From the depths of her pocket Ella produced a hanky for Lee to wipe her eyes on, and when the tearful little moment had passed she moved back to her chair and told Lee she was planning a party.

'I did think of a *MASH* party, but...' Ella wrinkled her nose. 'All that drab army gear! Then I had a brainwave! You know that lovely sequence out of *My Fair Lady*, at the races?'

'I do,' Lee said, and sang a couple of bars of the 'Ascot Gavotte'...

'Bravo! Well, that's the theme of my next party, and I think you could look as ravishing as Audrey Hepburn did, Lee!'

'Thank heavens you didn't choose *The Sound of Music*, Ella!' Damien said, coming into the room and sitting down next to Lee.

'Well…' Ella temporised. 'I did give it some—'

'She yodels,' Damien said, taking Lee's hand.

'I would never yodel in public!' Lee protested.

He pulled her into his arms. 'You've yet to yodel in private, but I'm still working on it.'

'Damien,' she whispered into his shoulder, unable to lift her head because she knew her cheeks were tinted bright pink.

He kissed the top of her head and tilted her chin to look into her eyes. 'Sweetheart,' he said softly. 'Sorry, I didn't mean to embarrass you. Just couldn't help it!'

And as Ella Patroni watched them at first she was amused, then her eyes widened and everything fell into place. She saw exactly how Lee filled the gap that had existed between Damien and Julia Blake-Whitney.

Obviously Lee was unaware of it, she mused, but did Damien know what had got to him about this girl? She suspected not, otherwise Lee would have no doubt as to his feelings…

She was tempted to put her thoughts into words, she even opened her mouth, but wisdom prevailed.

'You and Ella seem to get along pretty well,' Damien said, after Ella had left.

'Yes. I like her.'

'I would say she likes you,' he commented. 'Ella never bothers with people she doesn't like.' He looked at Lee wryly. 'She is also enormously curious. I'd be most surprised if she hadn't tried to pump you about our marriage.'

They were back in the bedroom and Damien was throwing clean clothes into his bag, having tossed all the clothes he'd taken to Vanuatu into a pile on the floor.

Lee picked up the bundle. 'I'll put these in the laundry. Do you have someone who comes in to clean and wash and iron?'

Damien took the bundle from her and dumped it on the floor again. 'Yes. Tell me about Ella.'

Lee backed away from him and sat down on the end of the bed. 'She... Damien, it was nothing! She said the mystery of it was driving them all crazy, that's...all.'

'You don't lie well, Lee.' He sat down beside her. 'Was it something that upset you?'

'No. And that's all I'm going to tell you,' she said composedly.

He paused. 'Why the mystery, though?'

She tilted her chin and eyed him through her lashes. 'I feel like being mysterious, that's all.'

'There are ways and means of dealing with that.' He laughed softly, and looked so wickedly alive she had no doubt as to his meaning.

'Don't even think of it,' she warned, however.

'Oh, not today,' he drawled. 'Three times in the space of one morning might be a bit much even for us. That doesn't mean to say I won't bide my time. I have some good news for you, by the way.'

She raised an eyebrow.

'It was Cosmo, the black sheep of the Delaney family, who pulled the scam on your grandparents.'

'*What?*' Lee blinked, her mouth fell open, then she said on a breath, 'Of course! The same initial, the resemblance— why didn't I think of that?'

'You had a lot on your mind?' he suggested gravely.

She went faintly pink. 'I guess so. But what made you suspect it?'

'Remember when we were having lunch at Byron Bay, you mentioned the resemblance between Cyril and Cosmo?'

She nodded.

'Well, right from the start it had me puzzled that Cyril should have a lookalike. When you said that, something clicked in my mind and I decided to have Cosmo investigated. In the course of it I turned up another claim against a

C. Delaney for a similar scam. And I've just got the news that Cosmo has a very dubious history.'

'Oh,' Lee breathed. 'Is that what Cyril suddenly suspected then left unsaid?'

'I would say so,' Damien agreed. 'Cyril had bailed him out a couple of times, apparently. But it seems likely that he decided to do things differently this time.'

'Because you are the son he never had and I...' She trailed off.

'Because you're who you are, Lee,' he said quietly. 'And because we've got to the state he foresaw for us. Haven't we?'

She was silent. Then, 'Wasn't it extremely dicey for Cosmo to reveal himself to me, though, since it was my grandparents—'

'There was no reason for him to connect the name of Westwood with Mercer, Lee.'

'Of course.'

'Also, in the course of these investigations, I came across their sister, Carol Delaney. She can't stand Cosmo. She thinks he's a disgrace to the family and would be more than happy to testify that Cyril and Cosmo were not close and had frequent arguments on the subject of Plover Park itself, in fact. Cosmo always wanted his brother to sell it.'

Lee's eyes widened. 'So...I see!'

'Yep! He never believed it belonged in the family, and he has no use for it himself. All he was after was the money it represents. And we have, have we not, Lee, fulfilled Cyril's dearest wish?'

She looked into his eyes and was shaken by the seriousness she saw. 'Yes...'

'Then let's go home.'

Three months later, Lee stopped what she was doing and burst into tears.

Damien had spent a week with her at Plover Park after

they'd come back from Vanuatu, and she'd been up to Brisbane a few times—Ella's party being one of them. Ella and Hank had also spent a few days at Plover Park. But otherwise she and Damien had only been together at weekends. And last night she'd got a call from Damien to say that he wouldn't be able to make it this weekend. The result was that she felt like a mistress, not a wife.

Which was not to say the weekends weren't wonderful, nor to say Damien didn't take a very active interest in Plover Park, he did. In fact he'd ensured that Lee's lifestyle was as pleasant as possible.

He'd had part of the shed converted into a flat, which he'd leased to a young couple who would act as caretakers when they were away—although that hadn't happened yet—and so that she was not totally alone at night. And he'd gone to some lengths to find the right couple, whose company she would enjoy without feeling hemmed in, and who could help with the heavy work.

He'd bought another dog to help Peach share the guard duties—a Great Dane puppy called Paddy that both Lee and Peach had fallen in love with. And he'd moved some of his brood mares and foals to Plover Park on discovering that Lee adored horses. He'd also bought a brand new four-wheel drive vehicle and trailer for the nursery, as well as converting one of the bedrooms into a study for her, with all the proper draughting tools for designing gardens.

And he'd instituted proceedings against Cosmo Delaney which looked like returning her grandparents' life savings to them. What more could he have done for her?

Nor could she say she wasn't busy doing what she loved, as more commissions rolled in. So why was she so desperately unhappy?

Because she felt as if she was tucked into a compartment of his life that didn't overlap into the rest of it.

Not that she was blameless. A couple of times he'd mentioned that they'd been invited to a party, would she like to come up for it? But something had always stopped her from agreeing. Some strange feeling that she was being pulled out of mothballs. Or perhaps a feeling that this marriage must still be a mystery to all his friends, and she didn't feel able to cope with their curiosity?

The only entertaining they did on the farm was for her grandparents, and the two solicitors who ran the Byron Bay branch of Moore & Moore and their wives. His mother had come down once for a weekend, and although she'd tried her best to cope with the new direction of her only son's marriage, Lee had not been able to detect any real warmth in Evelyn Moore.

The result was that his life during the week was a closed book to her. Their life, in fact, was a series of sensuous reunions that resembled an affair far more than a marriage. And he had made no mention of starting a family...

Peach butted her leg with his nose as she clung to a post and wept her heart out. So she sat down on the ground and buried her head in his silky coat. 'I was always afraid it would be a marriage of convenience, Peach,' she sobbed. 'But what to do about it? If I moved to Brisbane what would I do with myself?'

She lifted her head at last and looked around. Autumn was turning the landscape to old gold, leaves were fluttering to the ground as a sharp little breeze whistled through the trees and the clear sky was the deeper blue of approaching winter.

She shivered and wiped her eyes on the sleeve of her jumper. It came to her that she would do anything, even leave her beloved nursery and Plover Park if that was what it would take, to be a proper wife to Damien Moore. But was that what *he* wanted?

It was almost as if he had gone to extraordinary lengths to secure Plover Park for her—as compensation for the deficiencies in their marriage? she mused. The more she thought back, the more that seemed to leap out at her. What had he said the day they'd come back from Vanuatu? Something about how important Plover Park was to her...?

Not any more—how ironic! she thought sadly. So what to do? she wondered again. Make the best of things or try to explain her feelings to him?

The decision was taken out of her hands the very next day. She went to the dentist for her regular check-up and was paging through a magazine while she waited for her appointment. The back pages were the society pages. She looked uninterestedly through the Sydney and Melbourne social scene and was about to close it when a picture in the Brisbane section leapt out at her.

It was the Law Society's Annual Ball, she read with her heart in her mouth, only a couple of weeks ago, and pictured standing side by side in a laughing group were Damien and Julia Blake-Whitney. Damien looked breathtakingly handsome in a black tuxedo and Julia was stunning in a strapless violet gown that clung to her figure. She was also looking up at him in a clearly fascinated way.

The magazine fluttered to the floor from Lee's nerveless fingers and she got up and left, ignoring the startled receptionist's queries. And she drove home on auto-pilot, because all she could see was Julia's expression.

She left Plover Park that same day. She told her grandparents she was going to Brisbane for a week. She told the caretakers the same thing, and made sure they would take care of Peach and Paddy, the chickens and guinea fowl. But she told Lydia that she was very much afraid she wouldn't be back...

CHAPTER TEN

Two weeks later she was standing in front of the Sydney Opera House watching a glamorous array of guests arriving for a gala charity concert.

It was a chilly afternoon, heading towards dusk, and she'd been walking through the Domain and the Botanic Gardens.

She'd driven down to Sydney, taking her time, and found herself a pleasant motel to stay in while she contemplated her future—not that her thoughts had yielded much. In fact, she'd moved out of the motel that morning and had planned to drive south, but her car had developed a mysterious knock and she'd been forced to put it into a garage. It would be ready in an hour.

She was just about to turn away and find herself a warm café when Ella Patroni, magnificent in a full-length gold cape, with a real tiara adorning her head, stepped from a limousine, stopped as if shot, then with surprising agility, considering her bulk, pounced on Lee.

'My dear girl! *My dear girl!*' she crooned. 'Thank heavens I've found you! Damien is going out of his mind! Hank—' she turned imperatively '—forget about this! We've got much more important things to do! Get a car.'

Hank Patroni greeted Lee dazedly, then turned back to his wife. 'But—'

'Don't but me, Hank. How long have we known Damien Moore?' As she spoke, Ella hung on to Lee determinedly.

'Years,' Hank said. 'I was only about to say our limo has gone, Ella.'

'Then get another one!'

'I—' Lee started to say.

'And don't you give me any nonsense either, Lee,' Ella

broke in sternly. 'There—grab that one, Hank!' She pointed to a limo just about to depart.

Ten minutes later Lee was ensconced in the Patronis' lovely lamplit suite at the Regent, nursing a glass of brandy and soda.

'All right.' Ella discarded her cloak, took off her tiara and slung it on to a chair, causing Hank to look pained. 'Drink some of that,' she instructed Lee. 'You look as if you're about to faint. I'm not going to probe and pry into the whys and wherefores—I'm sure you have your reasons for what you did—but it was not fair to Damien to leave him without one word. Don't you agree, Hank?'

Poor Hank, Lee thought, and took a sip of her brandy.

'I…yes, I do,' Hank said slowly. 'He's not a monster, that much I do know, Lee.'

'I never thought he was.' Lee sipped some more brandy and felt some of the shock of it all recede. She'd taken off her anorak and was wearing a navy tracksuit beneath it. She looked away. 'But I didn't know what to say to him.'

'So the marriage of convenience came true.' Ella sat down beside Lee and put an arm around her. 'I wondered about that. You might find it's a different story now, Lee.'

Lee sniffed. 'All the same, if you could just let him know I'm alive and well. I did write to my grandparents, explaining. I couldn't seem to do it to their faces. But Damien—' She broke off, then realised that Ella was making peculiar signals to Hank, as if she was holding an imaginary phone to her ear. She sat up and said fervently. '*Please* don't ring him in Brisbane. I will get in touch, I promise—when I'm ready.'

Ella got up when Hank made no move, and picked up the phone. 'I'm only doing this,' she told Lee, 'because I believe it's the best for you both. I'm not one to sit idly by when my friends are in trouble.' Then she spoke into the phone and asked to be connected to a Mr Damien Moore.'

'What?' Lee whispered, and felt a roaring in her ears. 'No...'

'Damien?' Ella said into the phone. 'Could you pop up for a moment, right now? It's very important. Thanks.' She put the phone down and said to Lee, 'He's right here in this hotel. He came down on the same flight we did because he had a check done on the motels and your car registration came up, although you used a different name. So he would have found you anyway.'

She stopped as a knock sounded on the door and turned to Hank. 'That'll be him. Hank, we'll go to the concert. Hand me my tiara, please!' She drew her cloak on.

Hank got up resignedly. 'I hope you know what you're doing, Ella.'

Ella positioned her tiara, looked at them both regally, then swept out into the foyer.

Hank shrugged. 'He was terribly concerned, Lee. The reason we got to know about it was because he thought you might have got in touch with Ella. He was leaving no stone unturned, however unlikely.'

Not so unlikely, Lee thought. It had crossed her mind to get in touch with Ella...

'I...I...' she whispered, but Hank was gone and Damien had walked into the room.

Lee's first impression was that Ella had got it completely wrong. Rather than welcoming her back, Damien looked murderously angry as he came to stand in front of her in a dark suit and a blue and white striped shirt. He also looked tired, and thinner, with harsh lines scored beside his mouth.

His first words, as he watched her shrink back into the chair, did nothing to dispel the impression. 'If you ever do that to me again, Lee, I'll put you over my knee and spank the living daylights out of you.'

She gasped.

'Where the hell have you been? And what *insane* reason prompted you to...simply disappear?'

'I…it…I…' she stammered. 'It was the only thing I could think of to do! I just didn't want to be a…convenient wife any more, tucked away down on the farm while you lived two different lives. I should never have… I always knew you wanted a marriage of convenience, Damien, but you gave me so little choice.'

'I didn't live two different lives,' he grated. 'I worked when I wasn't with you.'

'You also socialised—'

'Which you refused to do on the occasions I couldn't get out of.'

'And you had Julia Blake-Whitney stand in for me,' she said huskily, her throat working. 'Who is still in love with you.'

He frowned. 'What the hell are you talking about?'

'I saw a picture in a magazine of the two of you at the Law Society Ball…'

For the first time there was a slight softening of those harsh lines beside his mouth. 'Is that why you ran away?' he said incredulously.

Lee hesitated and shrank further into her chair as he moved forward, but it was only her glass that he reached for. He poured them both a drink and sat down opposite her. He studied the contents of his glass for a long moment, then his dark lashes swept up and the hard glare had gone from his eyes. 'Is it, Lee?'

'Yes… One of the reasons.'

He sighed, but she got the curious feeling it was a sigh of relief. Then he said, 'She's a member of the Law Society too. I didn't go with her and it wasn't my doing that I ended up at the same table. I didn't go with anyone—the only reason I went at all is because I'm president this year. As to whether she's still in love with me, I have no idea. It makes no difference, though. But, yes, I'm guilty…of never understanding quite what it is I feel for you, Lee. And I'm guilty of not wanting to get too deeply involved in our marriage.'

Her lips parted.

'Or I was,' he said, looking down at his glass again, then suddenly up into her eyes. 'It was Ella who pointed out what had been lacking between Julia and me, and every other woman I've ever known. It was these two weeks that proved it once and for all.' He took a long draught of his drink. 'Especially this morning, when I discovered I'd missed you by a couple of hours.'

'What is it?' Lee asked, her eyes wide and very green with unshed tears.

He grimaced. 'You may not like it. I've barely slept…' He stopped, and for a moment looked utterly exhausted.

Lee sat forward at last, trembling all over but with a completely new sensation—hope. 'Do you love me or do you feel responsible for…*me* loving you?' she asked shakily.

'I can't bear the thought of any other man having you.'

'Damien—'

He smiled tiredly. 'You fascinate me, you make me feel incredibly good, you…' He paused, 'You arouse an instinct in me no other woman ever has. A protective instinct—I would slay dragons for you, Lee.'

She got up and went to kneel in front of him. 'Why…why wouldn't I like that, Damien?'

He went to touch her, then stopped himself. 'I got the feeling you were all the protection you thought you needed.'

'Damien,' she said softly, after a long moment, 'you mean my tiger mode?'

He nodded.

'That may have been how I dealt with the kind of person I thought Cyril Delaney was,' she said with a rueful little smile, 'but I have no protection against you and what you do to me. That was why I couldn't accept the… half-measure of our life together. It hurt too much.'

'Do you really mean that, Lee?'

'I thought you knew.'

'After Vanuatu, yes, but—'

'I fell in love with you long before Vanuatu, Damien,' she broke in. 'I fell in love with you right from the start.'

He blinked. 'How...?'

'How did I hide it? It wasn't easy,' she said sombrely. 'But I guess it helped to believe I wasn't the right one for you.'

He grimaced. 'You're more right than you could ever know—or I ever knew. These past few months haven't been easy for me either, Lee, but I've always had the greatest reservations about tearing you away from Plover Park. I've...never doubted your dedication to your career. I did doubt how I would measure up to it.'

She smiled through her tears and put her hand on his knee—their first contact. 'If I knew you loved me as much as I love you, there would never be any contest.'

He cupped her face and said barely audibly, 'Contrary to what I said when I stormed in here, I'd spend the rest of my life trying to get you back.' He shook his head and smiled, as if the joke was on him, 'I've gone from a bloke who couldn't really see the advantages of marriage to a staunch advocate of it—courtesy of you, Lee. A girl who reminded me of a one-woman SWAT team but turned out to be pure gold. What can I do to make you believe it?'

'Take me home,' she whispered. 'I love you.'

'Poor Hank,' Lee said, a lot later. 'He's been dragged away from the concert, then back to it. He won't know if he's on his head or his heels.'

'I'm sure he's used to it, but in fact I feel some sympathy for him.'

Lee moved in his arms. The closest to home they'd been able to get was to remove to his suite, after they'd ordered a bottle of champagne for Hank and Ella, and left a note saying that all was well propped against it. 'Not sure if *you're* on your head or your heels?' she asked.

He pulled her hard against him. 'Not sure this isn't a dream after all the nightmares. I may never be able to let you out of my sight. You know you told me you fell in love with me long before Vanuatu?'

Lee nodded wryly.

'I never could—really—understand why I decided to marry you. I'm not normally prone to quixotic gestures like that, so it's probably fair to say, Lee, that the same thing happened to me. Only I was too proud, too dumb, too arrogant—'

She stopped him by standing on her toes and kissing him. She felt him relax against her, then he slid his hands beneath her tracksuit top and murmured into her hair, 'You don't know how much I've missed doing this.'

'Taking my clothes off?'

'Precisely,' he agreed with a sudden wicked little glint in his eyes.

'I was…the same.'

'You once invited me to damn the consequences of this kind of intimacy—may I take it the invitation is still open, my lady?' he asked.

Lee smiled a little shyly up into his eyes. 'I did have something to prove then, remember?'

'So you did. And you proved it beautifully—I haven't been the same since. Is there anything you need to prove now?'

She took a deep breath. 'Only this. I had one other problem I didn't tell you about—I didn't even let myself dwell on it. But I'd love to have a baby—our baby.'

'To add to our collection of dogs, chooks, horses and guinea fowl?' he said humorously.

She looked suddenly anxious. 'Perhaps that's why I've got so many of them. I mean, I know I've had my grandparents, and they're wonderful, but sometimes I've felt such a loner in life, Damien, and—'

It was his turn to stop her by kissing her. 'I can think of nothing nicer, Lee.' He paused and looked around at the luxurious suite. 'Would this be a suitable place to set about…setting that in train?'

She looked around too and her lips quivered. 'I hope the Regent doesn't object, but so long as you're there a haystack, a paddock—anywhere you are—is fine with me.'

He laughed softly. 'You're right. I hope the walls don't have ears. OK, let's see what I can do.' He began to undress her, inflicting the kind of rapture on her she'd thought she might never experience again.

And all the pent-up hurt and sadness left her as he made love to her with the finesse that brought back so many memories: Erakor, Tamanu, Plover Park… But it was his reaction that overjoyed her. She felt, as they shuddered in each other's arms, that there had been a new hunger in him, almost desperate, and that had to be the result of two desperate weeks for him. And that kind of hunger had found an answering need in her, leaving her in no doubt that wherever they lived, whatever adjustments they made to their lives, the only two people in the world for them were each other.

He got up eventually, and brought her a glass of champagne. 'All right?'

She sipped the chilled drink and breathed deeply. 'Never better. Would you like me to prove it?'

He stared down at the gorgeous disarray of her hair, the lovely slender lines of her body, the faint blue shadows beneath her eyes that he was responsible for, the clear green depths of those eyes. 'Yes.'

She took another sip, and cleared her throat. Then she began to sing the first line of the 'The Lonely Goatherd' in a soft soprano, and she yodelled perfectly.

'Lee—' He started to laugh and then she was in his arms, regardless of her champagne which spilt all over them. 'I adore you!'

A few years later, she stood on the terrace of Plover Park holding a dark-haired little boy by the hand as they watched a helicopter hover over the paddock and then land.

'Daddy!' William Moore said excitedly. As he grew his vocabulary was starting to expand, but his first word had been 'Daddy' and his supreme hero went by the same name. 'Can I go, please? Please?'

Lee waited for a moment more, until the rotors had stopped and Damien had stepped out of the helicopter, then she released her son and watched him, with Paddy and Peach, run down towards the landing pad, scattering chickens and guinea fowl as they went.

And as she watched Damien sweep William up into his arms her thoughts moved backwards to that night at the Regent. Of course she couldn't be precisely sure, but she always liked to think she'd fallen pregnant that night. If not it had been very soon afterwards. The discovery of it had not only been momentous as an affirmation of their love, it had helped to sort out their lives for them.

Damien had suggested that they lease out the nursery, freeing her from the running of it but providing her with a source of plants so she could continue designing gardens. He'd also suggested that they move into the Ascot house, so she would have a garden, and his mother had been happy to move into his apartment.

But it was his acquisition of a helicopter, thereby considerably shortening the travel time it took to get from Brisbane, that had seen them able to spend a lot of time at Plover Park—most weekends, in fact, and often longer—and it brought her so much happiness to know that he loved the place as much as she did.

It was Ella Patroni who had suggested the means whereby Lee could be happy and fulfilled when she was away from Plover Park. She'd got Lee to redesign her roof garden and more commissions than Lee had dreamt possible had flowed from it. Not only roof gardens and terraces, even a commission to redesign a city park had come her way.

She'd moved into Damien's life more easily than she'd ever believed she could. Not only Ella had helped with that, but Evelyn Moore had finally overcome all her reservations and was now a firm ally.

But most of all Lee's transition from the girl who'd never thought she was the right one for Damien Moore to his wife, in every meaning of the word, had been accomplished by Damien himself.

She watched with her heart overflowing with love as her husband and her son approached—William talking nineteen to the dozen but Damien with his dark eyes fixed firmly on her. She and William had been on the farm for a week on their own while Damien had been to a conference in Sydney, but the short separations they often had to endure no longer bothered her.

She had William, and he adored the farm. His great-grandparents adored him, and his doting grandmother on his father's side was already talking about Lee not leaving it too long before she had another baby.

And Damien always came back to her with that hunger she'd sensed in him the night of their reunion.

But, as always, they restrained their passion until their son was asleep.

It was Damien who put him to bed that evening. Lee waited for him on the terrace, with a bottle of champagne in a silver frosted bucket, soft music playing and the flame of a candle moving like a genie in the soft night air—it was a special night tonight.

He dropped down into a chair beside her and reached for the champagne.

'Asleep?' she asked quietly as he removed the foil and popped the cork.

'I've never seen anyone avoid sleep as strenuously as he does,' he said wryly. 'But he just couldn't keep his eyes open a second longer.'

Lee laughed. 'It's you. His hero. My hero too.'

Damien poured the lovely bubbly liquid and handed her a glass.

'So, our wedding anniversary.'

'Mmm…what did you have in mind, Mr Moore?'

'Taking you to bed in a little while, undressing you very slowly, celebrating every gorgeous inch of you and making love to you in a celebration of this marriage. What do you think?'

Lee cast him a laughing look, but said honestly, 'I'm going hot and cold at the thought of it.'

'Then perhaps we shouldn't delay…things too long?'

'No,' she agreed, her voice suddenly husky as his dark gaze dwelt on her. Every nerve-ending she possessed tingled with sensation and desire swept through her like a flame. She swallowed. 'No. So I'll go first.'

She stood up and held her glass aloft to the night sky in the ritual they always practised on their wedding anniversary. 'To Cyril.'

'To Cyril,' Damien agreed, rising as well.

They drank, put their glasses down, and with love and laughter moved into each other's arms.

International bestselling author

SANDRA MARTON

invites you to attend the

WEDDING *of the* YEAR

Glitz and glamour prevail in this volume
containing a trio of stories in which
three couples meet at a
high society wedding—and
soon find themselves
walking down the aisle!

Look for it in November 2002.

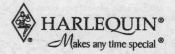

$ Saving Money $ Has Never Been This Easy!

Just fill out and send in this form from any October, November and December 2002 books and we will send you a coupon booklet worth a total savings of $20.00 off future purchases of Harlequin and Silhouette books in 2003.

Yes! It's that easy!

**I accept your incredible offer!
Please send me a coupon booklet:**

Name (PLEASE PRINT)

Address   Apt. #

City   State/Prov.   Zip/Postal Code

**In a typical month, how many
Harlequin and Silhouette novels do you read?**

❏ 0-2   ❏ 3+

097KJKDNC7   097KJKDNDP

Please send this form to:
In the U.S.: Harlequin Books, P.O. Box 9071, Buffalo, NY 14269-9071
In Canada: Harlequin Books, P.O. Box 609, Fort Erie, Ontario L2A 5X3

Allow 4-6 weeks for delivery. Limit one coupon booklet per household. Must be postmarked no later than January 15, 2003.

HARLEQUIN®
Makes any time special®

Silhouette®
Where love comes alive™

If you enjoyed what you just read,
then we've got an offer you can't resist!

Take 2 bestselling love stories FREE!

Plus get a FREE surprise gift!

Clip this page and mail it to Harlequin Reader Service®

IN U.S.A.	**IN CANADA**
3010 Walden Ave.	P.O. Box 609
P.O. Box 1867	Fort Erie, Ontario
Buffalo, N.Y. 14240-1867	L2A 5X3

YES! Please send me 2 free Harlequin Presents® novels and my free surprise gift. After receiving them, if I don't wish to receive anymore, I can return the shipping statement marked cancel. If I don't cancel, I will receive 6 brand-new novels every month, before they're available in stores! In the U.S.A., bill me at the bargain price of $3.57 plus 25¢ shipping & handling per book and applicable sales tax, if any*. In Canada, bill me at the bargain price of $4.24 plus 25¢ shipping & handling per book and applicable taxes**. That's the complete price and a savings of at least 10% off the cover prices—what a great deal! I understand that accepting the 2 free books and gift places me under no obligation ever to buy any books. I can always return a shipment and cancel at any time. Even if I never buy another book from Harlequin, the 2 free books and gift are mine to keep forever.

106 HDN DNTZ
306 HDN DNT2

Name	(PLEASE PRINT)	
Address	Apt.#	
City	State/Prov.	Zip/Postal Code

 * Terms and prices subject to change without notice. Sales tax applicable in N.Y.
** Canadian residents will be charged applicable provincial taxes and GST.
   All orders subject to approval. Offer limited to one per household and not valid to
   current Harlequin Presents® subscribers.
   ® are registered trademarks of Harlequin Enterprises Limited.

PRES02   ©2001 Harlequin Enterprises Limited